Mr

ng

... rang your dad and myself on Friday ...ernoon.'

'But Dunky had had his turn at the parents' evening. He can't call you as well. That's cheating!' I was outraged.

'Mr Duncan is very concerned about you. Especially after you told him that since you started vlogging you can't sleep at night.'

'That's rubbish,' I replied.

'It's exactly what you told Mr Duncan, isn't it, Louis? Tell the truth.'

I felt myself going red, right to my ears.

'So you realise that what we're going to do is not because you've done anything wrong.'

An ice-cold shiver ran right through me …

and the **Louis** ᴛ... ...

'In Louis, Pete Johnson has created a
boy who makes you laugh out loud.'
Sunday Times

'Pete Johnson is a wonderful storyteller.'
Evening Standard

'Fast, funny, and very readable.'
Carousel

'A rip-roaringly hilarious adventure.'
The Book Trust

'Funny and light ... the humour disguises
real emotional truth and depth.'
The Guardian

'A great story for boys and girls alike.'
The School Librarian

'This is such a brilliant book!'
'My daughter LOVED this book.'
'JUST BUY IT. YOU WILL NOT REGRET IT.'
'The best book I've ever read.'
Amazon.co.uk reviews

How to Fool Your Parents

Pete Johnson

AWARD PUBLICATIONS LIMITED

ISBN 978-1-78270-247-4

Text copyright © 2016 Pete Johnson
Illustrations by Nikalas Catlow
This edition copyright © Award Publications Limited

First published by Award Publications Limited 2017

Published by Award Publications Limited,
The Old Riding School, Welbeck,
Worksop, S80 3LR

www.awardpublications.co.uk

17 1

Printed in the United Kingdom

*The book is dedicated to Valerie Christie
– a truly inspiring librarian, whose
support means so much.*

Chapter One

Power Nap

Tuesday February 25th

4.30 p.m.

I'd like to make a full confession.

I, Louis – full name Louis the Laugh – did, at approximately 3.45 p.m. today, say, 'Sir, I am so incredibly sorry and I would like to volunteer for an extra detention right here, right now.'

Am I ashamed of myself? Totally. But I had no choice. You see, I'm in an incredibly desperate situation. No, really … Just hear me out.

It was the last lesson of the day, physics. Yawn! It was with Mr Duncan (known to all as Dunky). Double yawn.

7

Well, I was feeling drowsier and drowsier. But I really only meant to rest my eyes for a moment. Most unfortunately my head then slipped down onto my chest ...

A power nap is the technical term for what happened next. And if Dunky had left me alone I'd have woken up all refreshed – and ready to learn more. Instead he hissed down my ear, 'You can't sleep in my class.'

'If you didn't speak so loudly I could,' was what I longed to reply. But I knew this was a moment which required tact. So I tried to explain that I'd only taken a very brief power nap. And they are actually very popular these days.

But he wasn't listening. Instead sarcasm dripped from him as he creaked, 'I'm very glad you've decided to re-join us. Your contributions to the class are so vital' – the class all chortled away at this (I never say a word in his lessons) – 'and I will see you at the end of the lesson to discuss your sleeping arrangements.'

And later, while everyone else escaped, I approached Dunky, smiling bravely. He rose up from his desk. He's very tall and immensely thin, with a long but somehow scrunched-up face, a truly mouldy grey beard and the tiniest eyes you've ever seen – like two little raisins glaring down at you.

But here's what you need to know. I had to somehow get on Dunky's good side, as I needed him to do me a massive favour. A truly hopeless mission you might think, and you'd be right. But I had to achieve the impossible.

That's why, when he announced that I had a double detention tomorrow, I gushed, 'Thank you so much, Mr Duncan, I so deserve it.' Then I uttered the words I told you about before and I can't bear to repeat ever again.

And guess what Dunky said after my truly amazing offer. Nothing. He merely pointed a gnarled hand at the desk in front of him.

And ever since, I have been sitting here, filling page after page with lines. And I didn't stop once – well, not until he tottered off for a moment.

HOLD UP. He's coming back.

More soon.

4.50 p.m.

I proudly took my lines up to Dunky. 'Five and a half pages there,' I said. 'And no hardship at all. Just happy to be here with you.' He hardly even glanced at what I'd written. Yes, a bit rude but I knew why. He was still annoyed about me dropping off in his lesson, wasn't he? And as one performer to another I could understand that. It makes you feel you're not gripping your audience, for a start.

So I said, 'I want to assure you, Mr Duncan, your lesson wasn't any more boring than usual. I mean, it wasn't boring at all,' I added hastily. 'In fact, it was fascinating. Especially ...' I tried to remember one thing he'd said and couldn't, so spluttered, 'Well, there were so many highlights I can't just pick one.' Then I smiled winningly at him.

Not a flicker from him. Blankly is the best word to describe how Dunky was scrutinising me. Yet somehow I had to win over this dry husk of a teacher in his crumpled grey suit who skulked about the school like a sinister ghost.

But how?

It seemed I had no choice. I was going to have to take him into my confidence.

So I asked him, 'Sir, would you like to know the real reason I fell asleep in your lesson?'

Was there the tiniest flicker of interest in those tiny eyes? Anyway, he nodded, but extremely slowly like a toy which urgently needed winding up.

'You may know, sir, my ambition is to be a comedian. And that I appeared on satellite television recently for three whole minutes telling jokes on my friend Poppy's show. Perhaps you even saw me,' I added hopefully.

'No,' he snapped.

'Ah, never mind. Anyway, after that I was invited onto a vlog. Do you know what they are?'

'No,' he snapped again.

'Well, don't feel bad, I bet loads of people in their riper years haven't a clue either. They're videos made by teenagers who then put them up on the internet.' I had my doubts that Dunky even knew what the internet was.

'Anyway, the most popular vlog right now is hosted by Noah and Lily. They've got nearly ten million followers. Just imagine that.' I paused briefly to allow Dunky to do just that. 'So you can imagine how excited I was to be invited onto their show.'

But I had a feeling I was losing Dunky so I rushed on, 'Anyway, I was invited on there to help kids with their problems, and to be funny as well. And would you believe it, I was such a big hit I've been invited back this Sunday. I hardly slept last night I was so happy and that's why I needed a tiny power nap in your lesson.'

That was a lie actually, as I slept perfectly last night even though I am insanely excited about Sunday. But that's me, always trying to spread good cheer and lift people's spirits. 'So you see, my little nap had nothing to do with you, sir,' I said. 'I bet that's cheered you up. And I'd be so grateful if you could do me a favour now.'

Dunky's eyebrows almost shot off his head.

'You know tonight is a parents' evening, and my mum and dad and I will be trotting along to hear your words of wisdom. Well, of course I want you to feel free to talk about anything you like. Only I'd be incredibly happy if you wouldn't mention my very brief power nap in your lesson, as news like that can do terrible things to parents' minds, especially highly impressionable ones like mine. They might do something drastic – even stop me appearing on Noah and Lily's vlog this Sunday.'

Surely even Dunky could see that a return appearance on the vlog was such an extraordinary and fantastic opportunity.

'In return, I'll do as many detentions as you want. Plus, I'll pick up litter after school.' Teachers love you doing this, don't they? 'You name it, I'll do it. And I know I'll be in your debt.' I'd heard someone say that last sentence in a film once and I liked it so much I repeated it very slowly. 'I'll … be … in … your … debt, Mr Duncan.'

Dunky slowly, jerkily, got to his feet. (He always moves like a life-sized puppet.)

'I am, of course, happy to carry your bag to

the car now as well.' I threw that in because I was getting desperate. I had a horrible feeling I hadn't won Dunky over.

But then he actually gave me a tiny smile as he whispered – he never ever raises his voice – 'I am looking forward to meeting your parents tonight.'

'It's a big night for them too,' I grinned.

'I have so much to tell them,' Dunky said gravely.

He left without another word.

I'm not quite sure what he meant.

But I'd say things look bad, don't they?

Very bad.

Chapter Two

Keeping My Parents Laughing

5.10 p.m.
What should I do now?

a) Tell Mum and Dad the parents' evening has been postponed.
Unfortunately my parents – and especially my mum – have deeply suspicious natures. And, very shockingly, they wouldn't just take my word for it. They'd also demand reasons for it being postponed, and I can't think of a single one.

*   *   *

b) Say Dunky turned up today dressed as the Easter Bunny.

Tell them the school is trying to hush up the fact that he has gone off his nut. He may well say the wildest things tonight, and if I warn my parents just to act as if they agree with him to avoid another episode, I might just get away with it. Maybe?

c) Lie shivering in bed with the curtains drawn and uttering blood-curdling moans.

I have a definite flair for being ill. Unfortunately I have done this so many times already I doubt that even my truly superb acting would convince my parents again. And anyway they might still go without me.

d) Get my story in first.

Explain with a merry laugh that I took the teeniest power nap in Dunky's lesson. Then warn them how Dunky will try to make it sound as if I settled down in a sleeping bag for several weeks.

I wouldn't normally have considered this option for a second. But recently my parents have changed – for the better.

It all started when Dad landed a job interview

(he'd been out of work for months). Night after night he and Mum prepared for it. Anyway, Dad did the interview and was offered the job.

Since then he and Mum have been busily getting ready for his first day. Which is today. They have also given up all their bad habits.

So they haven't asked me once about my homework or how I got on at school. They haven't even mentioned tonight's parents' evening.

Actually they've hardly spoken to me at all. So they've transformed into perfect parents really.

They've also been in an incredibly good mood all the time.

So could I risk slipping them the info about my little nap? Will they be so caught up in Dad's first day that they'll hardly react?

Or will it start a relapse?

Only one person will know what I should do now: Maddy.

Maddy is my agent and girlfriend – only I haven't seen her for three weeks and three days. We haven't broken up. It's even worse than that. No, it isn't. Nothing could be worse than us breaking up. It is pretty bad though.

Her family have moved to America. California, to be precise. Burlingate in California, to be even more precise.

I act as if it's dead cool having a girlfriend/

agent living right next to Hollywood. Maddy even had some swanky cards made, which I hand round with merry abandon.

But actually I hate her being so far away and I'd give anything to have her living three roads away from me again. Especially as Maddyland is eight hours behind us.

So right now, Maddy has just arrived at school. And by the time she's back home it's late evening here and I've had to hand over my phone for the night.

Hopeless!

Except for the fact that Maddy's parents have signed a practically legal contract promising she can come home for every single holiday.

And whenever I leave a message for Maddy to call me, she always does. Really quickly too.

You'll see ...

5.40 p.m.
Told you.

Maddy has just rung me – from the girls' loo.

She asked, 'Is it unusual, Louis, that your mum and dad haven't mentioned this parents' evening at all?'

'Highly unusual.'

'You don't think they could have completely forgotten all about it?'

My stomach did a flip. 'Hey, wouldn't that be a result?'

'So why don't you suggest,' went on Maddy, 'you all go out for a meal tonight to celebrate your dad's new job?'

'Great idea, keep them distracted ... but what if they do remember about tonight? Do I spill the beans about me nodding off for a few seconds before they meet Dunky?'

'No. After all, Dunky might not tell them. You don't know for certain. Much better to keep your mum and dad laughing all the time. Then no teacher – not even Dunky – can bring them down. It won't be easy.'

'It certainly won't.'

Then I heard American voices in the background and Maddy just had time to add, 'Very few people could do it, Louis. But you can.'

6.15 p.m.

Dad is back and chuffed to bits. He has got his own office (even though he is only there part-time).

'Hey, Dad, you're back all right!' I yelled.

That's when Dad suddenly high-fived me.

'You know what we should do – go out and celebrate your new job tonight,' I went on.

'Well, there is this new restaurant I've been

18

hearing great things about on—' Dad stopped. 'But Elliot is away at a sleepover.' (Elliot is my midget brother.)

'Even better,' I shouted eagerly, 'as we won't have to watch him shovelling food into his gullet. Call that restaurant now before it gets booked up!'

Dad was actually dialling the restaurant when Mum appeared. He beamed at her. 'Thought we deserved a celebratory meal out.'

'Wonderful ... but isn't it Louis's parents' evening tonight?' She looked at me questioningly.

I shrugged extremely vaguely. 'Not sure ... could be ... I don't think so.'

'No, it is,' said Mum.

Dad stopped dialling, then shook himself like someone waking up. 'Do you know, I'd completely forgotten about that.'

'So had I, for a moment,' admitted Mum.

'Well, go on forgetting about it,' I cried, 'as it'll only bring the mood right down. And you two so deserve a good night out.'

Do you know, Dad actually hesitated? He looked at Mum. 'I suppose there's no way we could miss it just this once?'

She shook her head, but more than a bit sadly.

'Look,' I cried, 'I can tell you in one sentence what all my teachers will say about me: "Louis is a truly massive doughnut." There, you've heard it all. Now, Dad, get dialling as I'm starving.'

Suddenly Mum was looking right at me. 'You're very keen for us not to go.'

'Only because I'm thinking of you two. And I don't want you to spend tonight sitting on the hardest chairs known to humanity in miserable, pokey classrooms, which all smell of stale cabbage—'

'Oh, Louis, your classrooms are nothing like that,' interrupted Mum, laughing. 'And you never know, your teachers might surprise you.'

'And we'll definitely have that meal another night,' said Dad.

He and Mum went, grinning, into the kitchen. They were both still in exceptionally chilled moods.

Somehow I've got to keep them that way.

7.15 p.m.
At school we were confronted by a wall of parents and their unfortunate sprogs massing down corridors that ponged of polish. First teacher on our list was Mrs Hare, my form teacher.

'I'll just warn you,' I hissed, 'not to stare too long at Mrs Hare's luxurious moustache. It could win prizes.'

Dad smothered a laugh. I'd had him and Mum

giggling all the way here.

Mrs Hare had opened all the windows in her lair, so it was like entering an icebox. She was sitting in front of the whiteboard, her moustache blowing gently in the wind. She was a small, dumpy-looking woman wearing a necklace – which looked like it could double as a bottle opener. She tries her hardest to be positive about everyone – yes, even me.

'Well now ... Louis,' she began. 'He's ... he's ...' She was really struggling to think of something good to say about me. 'He's ...' she squeaked desperately.

'A total genius,' I prompted.

Mrs Hare gave a nervous laugh. 'You're certainly quite a character.' She turned to my parents. 'But I'm afraid Louis can be very chatty.'

TRANSLATION: I never stop talking.

'And some subjects don't come naturally to him.'

TRANSLATION: I'm bottom in everything.

'While his homework is inconsistent.'

TRANSLATION: I don't do any homework.

'So what I'd like Louis to do,' she continued, 'is work on his emergent strengths.'

'Oh, what are they?' asked Mum eagerly. And she and Dad both leaned forward.

'They are …' Mrs Hare thought so hard. 'Well, none have actually appeared yet – but I'm sure they will when Louis takes more responsibility for his own learning.'

TRANSLATION: When Louis actually does some work.

Next she rattled off something about target levels and sub levels, which I don't think even Mum understood, and then our time was up.

'Well, it's good I've got all these emergent strengths,' I said afterwards, 'even if no one actually knows what they are.'

Dad gave a feeble little chuckle.

We'd only seen one teacher. And the nicest! But already my parents were drooping. The fun was leaking out of them. So what on earth will they be like after they've seen the next teacher on our list?

Dunky.

'Now,' I said. 'We can either go and visit a man with a face like a decaying potato, who is just shy of a hundred, or have a mighty refreshing cup of coffee which is completely free … I'd say it was a no-brainer.'

'Let's get it over with,' said Mum briskly.

But even she recoiled when she peered inside Dunky's classroom. It was in total darkness, save for one dim light. You could just make out

Dunky sitting completely still at his desk.

'Before we go in,' I whispered, 'do you think we should all hold hands?'

Dad let out such a loud laugh Mum had to shush him, but even her shoulders were starting to shake. I'd made them happy again – for now.

Mum knocked on the door and said softly, 'Now, come on, everyone, behave.'

'And look out for any bats,' I whispered.

Dad chuckled again.

And Dunky, in his best dark suit, did look as if he was auditioning to be the next Count Dracula. He greeted Mum and Dad with a mothballed courtesy. Then he glared in my direction as if I were a stinky smell which had wafted in with them.

To think we could have been having a fantastic meal out now instead of being trapped in a stuffy torture chamber with Dunky. He talked a bit about the syllabus, and then he smacked his lips appreciatively. 'I have to tell you I am extremely concerned about Louis's progress. Especially after something very troubling which occurred only this afternoon.'

Here it comes, I thought. The moment when Dunky changes my parents back into the super-stressy, never-off-my-back ones again. Parents who are so anxious and concerned they could do anything, even stop me appearing on a top vlog this Sunday. And there was nothing I could do to stop it.

For the second time that day I closed my eyes in Dunky's classroom.

And that's when it happened.

Chapter Three

Saved by a Tooth

It gave me quite a start.

I was chewing a toffee, to calm my nerves. But as I chomped I gulped nervously in anticipation of my impending doom, and the sweet quickly disappeared down my slightly surprised throat. The toffee was gone, but there was an odd taste in my mouth. And something else.

Something that felt exactly like a massive crater where one of my teeth should be.

The next thing I knew blood was oozing out of my mouth. No wonder I let out a small yelp. The kind a highly bewildered Jack Russell might make. And, by the sheerest coincidence, this was just as Dunky was about to tarnish my name.

'Is something wrong, Louis?' asked my mum, more than a bit sharply, I thought.

'Oh no ... It's just my mouth seems to be bleeding quite a lot, that's all,' I said. 'Anyone got a spare hankie to help soak up all the blood?'

Dad sprang up and started rooting about for a handkerchief before Mum got up and handed me one.

I took it and started to dab at my mouth, just as something fell out into my hand. And it wasn't a giant stone at all. I peered down at it. 'I think one of my teeth has made a bid for freedom,' I said. 'But it'll be fine. Don't call for an ambulance or anything. If I just sit here quietly I'm sure the bleeding will stop – eventually.'

Mum and Dad both sat down again. And Mum actually apologised to Dunky. Don't ask me what for.

Then Dunky said in a distinctly peeved voice, 'If I might be allowed to continue.'

'Yes, please keep going,' I said bravely. 'Don't anyone bother about my health.'

'What I was about to say—' he began.

But I was determined he wasn't going to say another word. So I let out another louder cry. 'Apologies for that,' I said, 'but I am in quite a lot of torment, what with me still swallowing gallons of blood and feeling incredibly weak. In fact, I think I might be about to pass out.'

Mum and Dad leapt up again.

'Everything's gone very faint,' I murmured.

Mum came over and took my hand for a moment. 'You have gone rather hot,' she said.

How lucky was that? 'Feel very hot too,' I gasped. 'But please carry on. The pain isn't *too* bad.'

Mum and Dad finally sat down again. By now Dunky's next victim and his family were peering through the glass.

'Aargh! Aargh!' I cried, and then I added, 'Sorry, I'll try to suffer more quietly.'

Dunky hissed, more than a bit crossly, 'I suppose we'll have to leave it there. For now.'

I felt like leaping about the room and cheering. But instead I tottered slowly out of his room while clutching my bloodied jaw. The waiting family gawped at me in alarm. 'Just don't get Mr Duncan angry and you'll be fine,' I whispered.

I was allowed to escape to the loo. Actually the bleeding had already stopped, but I hung about for ages and ages. I finally struggled out and wheezed, 'I'm sure the agony will stop quite soon now.'

We missed my next appointment and a good half of the following one and my parents were distracted for the rest of the evening.

It was only later, at home, that Mum asked me, 'I wonder what the very troubling thing that Mr Duncan was going to talk to us about was.'

'All right, Mum, I'll tell you,' I said. 'He thinks I breathe too loudly.'

'What!' exclaimed Mum and Dad together.

'Or something like that. *Talking of monsters, what game do they like best? Hide and shriek.*'

'That's a terrible joke,' cried Mum.

'Here's an even worse one. *What soup do vampires like best? Scream of mushroom.*'

'Enough,' laughed Dad. And soon he was telling us some more about his new office and Mum was looking thrilled to see him so happy again.

And do you know, not another word was said about the parents' evening.

9.02 p.m.
Told Maddy the good news and she has just texted:

Fate is really smiling on you and I know why. Great things are about to come your way.

I immediately texted back:

If fate really wanted to make me happy you'd be coming home.

Still, I think Maddy could be right. Great things are about to come my way. And I believe it will all start on Sunday with my return to Noah and Lily's vlog.

But my parents are not completely out of danger yet.

Would you believe another parents' evening is breaking out tomorrow at Elliot's school. Even more incredibly, Elliot is thicker than me.

So Mum and Dad still need very special attention.

It's just lucky I already have a plan.

Chapter Four

The Perfect Son

Wednesday February 26th

8.18 a.m.
Only Mum and Dad are invited to Elliot's parents' evening so I will have to look after Freaky Features while they are away. Normally such news would be enough to make me lose my breakfast. But I need my little brother's help this evening. So I just said smoothly, 'No problem at all, Mum.'

She immediately pretended to fall over with shock. She really should leave the jokes to me.

* * *

6.25 p.m.

The very second Mum and Dad depart I announce, 'Right, Elliot, we're going to be very busy.'

'Doing what?' he demanded.

'Well, cleaning ...'

'I'm not cleaning anything.'

'You so are. And I'll tell you why. When Mum and Dad return home, what sort of mood do you suppose they'll be in?'

Elliot shrugged. 'I don't know.'

'Take a wild guess.'

'A really rubbish one,' he said at last. Then he blurted out, 'I don't think parents' evenings should be allowed.'

'I totally agree with you. What happens at school stays at school. But right now our parents will be hearing how totally useless you are, so we've got to fool them into thinking you're not. We do this by cleaning the whole house and having the smell of coffee wafting in the air when they arrive. Plus ...' I scrutinised him. 'Somehow you have got to be revoltingly cute. I think you should be in pyjamas and rush right up to them, saying, "I'm not too old for a hug, am I?"'

'I've got to say *that*?' gasped Elliot.

'And then you'll have to shower them with

big, sloppy kisses.'

Elliot let out a huge sigh. 'Sometimes I hate my life.'

8.25 p.m.
Mum and Dad stumbled in. 'Hello, boys,' said Mum in a sort of strangled voice before tottering to the sofa and sagging onto it.

Dad actually brushed a bead of perspiration from his brow, before he flopped down beside her. 'Louis, we thought your parents' evening was bad – what we saw of it, anyway – but tonight ...' His anguished voice fell away.

'It's all over now,' I said soothingly. 'Take a few deep breaths and you'll be fine.'

But I was angry on their behalf. It's not right to inflict all this torture on them. If only teachers would stop and think about the impact of their words. We pupils can take it. But parents are not made of such strong stuff. It was definitely time to start on my plan.

So I announced loudly, 'There's someone upstairs who specially wanted to stay up and see you.'

Elliot, who had been waiting for my signal, came tumbling down the stairs. 'Welcome home,' he cried excitedly as if they'd been away for two years not two hours. 'I'm not too old for a hug, am I?'

'Of course not, love,' replied Mum. 'But is anything wrong?'

'Yes,' whispered Elliot.

'Tell us,' urged Mum.

'I so missed you not being here tonight, that's all. It just didn't feel like home. Instead there was this great empty space,' whispered Elliot, energetically hugging them both and throwing in squishy kisses, exactly as I'd instructed.

I watched Little Legs with undisguised pride – I'd taught him well – until Mum started to cough. 'What on earth is that smell?'

'Elliot does stink ...' I began apologetically.

'No, in the house,' said Mum.

'I can smell it too,' said Dad.

I beamed at them both. 'We've been doing some cleaning.'

Actually Elliot and I argued so much about who was going to clean what that we never actually got round to doing anything. But we did spray, highly energetically, tons of stuff about to give the house an incredibly clean feel.

'And I hope you've also been able to smell coffee,' I declared. This was Elliot's signal to spring off and fetch it. He reappeared, only managing to spill half of it before handing it round and saying, 'Hope this puts you out of your misery.'

'What he meant,' I quickly jumped in, 'is that he knows what miserable places schools are.'

'This coffee is really quite good,' murmured Dad.

'Only the best for you two.' Then I put on the CD of ABBA's 'Dancing Queen'. 'I remember you singing this in the car, Mum, just after you'd been to see *Mamma Mia*.'

'And I remember how highly embarrassed you were,' said Mum.

'But I'm so much more mature these days,' I replied. 'And now I see there's nothing wrong with old – er, older – people enjoying themselves when no one else is watching. So drink your coffee and sing along.' Then I slipped upstairs. A few minutes later I returned. 'All right, Mum, I have run a bath for you.'

'You have?' She looked both startled and pleased.

'I used that lavender bath oil you like so much. And I have lit a few candles just to add to the atmosphere. So you can go upstairs now and have a good old soak.'

'I feel as if I've checked into a five-star hotel, Louis,' cried Mum.

'Just call me the perfect son,' I replied humbly.

9.08 p.m.

Mum is back downstairs after her bath. She and Dad are smiling again. They're still coughing quite a lot too. We really did overdo the fresh clean smells.

But guess what – they haven't mentioned Elliot's parents' evening again.

It's been a nerve-jangling couple of days. My parents could so easily have slipped back to their very bad old ways.

But I'd say they are now out of danger.

Chapter Five

Edgar the Terrible

Thursday February 27th

5.10 p.m.
Elliot has just pranced into my room. 'I love you, Louis,' he said, wrapping his arms round me. Then he let out a truly ear-splitting fart. It just exploded out of him.

'What is wrong with your insides?' I demanded.

Elliot could hardly stand up from laughing. I should have pulverised him, but I didn't because I was sort of grinning too.

Of course, making a stink is the very lowest form of humour. Much better is to make people laugh with a joke like:

Which king had a noisy bottom?
Richard the Lionfart.

I have a talent (my only one) for making people smile.

So I loved telling jokes on television when my friend Poppy gave me a guest slot on her Christmas show. And I'm pretty certain I'll be invited back soon. That's why I practise telling jokes in front of the mirror every single night. I'm also re-reading the funniest book I've ever read, *Joy in the Morning* by P.G. Wodehouse, and this time I'm even making notes. (Yes, honestly!)

Plus, looking down from my walls is every genius comedy character you can think of. In fact, this is not really a bedroom, more a cave of funniness.

Friday February 28th

You know how I've worked my fingers to the bone entertaining my parents? Well, tonight I decided I'd take a well-earned breather.

But then I saw Mum stalking about the kitchen looking all miserable. Later Dad joined her and they started whispering together. I couldn't quite hear what they were saying, but

I had a feeling I knew exactly what they were talking about.

Parents' evenings.

I wanted to say to them, 'Come on, let's put this behind us. Think of all the things you've got to look forward to, like your son about to appear on a vlog watched by nearly ten million people.'

But instead I sat down with the two gloom buckets and told them joke after joke. After a bit Dad laughed, and finally even Mum cracked a smile.

But I can't spend all my time cheering up their lives, can I?

Saturday March 1st

6.25 p.m.
Maddy's just told me off.

'When I left, you promised me you'd go and see Edgar.'

'I didn't exactly promise.'

'Louis, you so did.'

Edgar is unique – uniquely awful. A thirteen-year-old who acts as if he's eighty-six. He's too clever for school, so he has a tutor instead. He's also Maddy's only other client. You see, he writes poetry – some of which Maddy even persuaded the local paper to feature.

'I'm worried about him,' said Maddy. 'He sounds a bit strange.'

'That's because he *is* a bit strange.'

'No, I don't think he's very happy.'

'He never is,' I said.

'You must go and see him today.'

'But why?' I wailed. 'I haven't done anything wrong.'

'Louis, please do this for me,' said Maddy.

So now I'm off to see Edgar the Terrible. And that's a sentence I never thought I'd write.

7.15 p.m.

Got a huge surprise when I rolled up at Edgar's massive house. When I appeared on the doorstep the front door sprang open and this elderly lady practically flung her arms around me.

'I know exactly who you are,' she beamed.

Had Maddy texted Edgar to say that I was on my way? Or maybe she had seen me on television on Poppy's show? I hoped so. It's great to have fans of all ages.

'I'm Edgar's nan and looking after him while his parents are away,' she beamed at me. 'I know Edgar will be so happy to see you again.'

This was news to me. He and I have never exactly been big mates. Not mates at all, in fact. But yet, he'd been waiting all these weeks for me to call. He clearly had better taste than I thought.

She added, 'You haven't brought anything with you.'

So she was obviously expecting me to bring Edgar a present. Bit cheeky. He's not six.

'Never mind,' she went on, escorting me through a posh-looking hallway. 'Edgar has so much to show you.'

Now I was confused, and even a bit worried. What was Edgar going to show me? Not his poems – please, not that!

'Edgar first got interested in rocks when he stayed with me,' she went on. 'I lived by the sea then.'

'Ah, I see,' I said, although I didn't. I just knew this conversation was getting weirder and weirder.

She led me into the sitting room where logs crackled in the big fireplace. Seated beside the fire, in a large armchair, was Edgar. He was holding in his hand something that glinted and sparkled.

A rock.

Many more of them were displayed in a case on the table beside Edgar, like exhibits at a museum.

'Look who's here. I told you he'd call, didn't I?

Well, I'll leave you both to chat. Make yourself at home, Tim.'

Tim! Why on earth had she called me that? It doesn't sound anything like Louis.

Edgar looked up, his floppy blond fringe almost hiding his starey blue eyes. And just for a second, a flash of disappointment crossed his face. Then he returned to scrutinising his rocks. 'You're not Tim,' he announced to the table.

'I didn't think I was, but thanks for confirming. Who is he anyway?'

'This boy I met at a science lecture, who also collects rocks. When I told Mum about him she insisted on inviting him round for tea. Bombarded him with texts, in fact. But I knew he wouldn't turn up. And what are you doing here anyway? Oh, don't tell me, Maddy sent you to check up on me. Why can't everyone realise I like being on my own? It's my choice. Tell her that.'

'Tell her yourself. So, what are you up to? Still writing poetry?'

'Of course.'

'Can I see any of it?' I asked. I even put an interested look on my face and you can't ask for more than that.

'No,' he snapped.

'That's a relief,' I grinned. Then I added,

'Do you ever look at people's faces when you're talking to them?'

'I did try looking at people's faces once,' replied Edgar, 'but I didn't like it.'

I laughed, even though I didn't think he was trying to be funny. 'So why do you like rocks so much?' I asked chattily.

'You wouldn't understand.'

'I might, if you speak very slowly.'

Edgar shook his head in such a snooty, dismissive way I really wanted to wallop him.

'Ready for your tea now, boys?' Yes, that smiley nan was back. 'Come and sit down and make yourselves comfortable, Tim. I hope you like—'

'Nan, Tim isn't coming,' interrupted Edgar wearily.

'But ... but ...' She stared at Edgar and then at me. 'But he's here.'

'No, this isn't Tim,' said Edgar.

Now she was looking at me quite indignantly. 'But why on earth did you pretend you were?'

There are moments – when I'm extremely nervous – when I start gabbling away in an Australian accent. Haven't done it for ages but right then I burst out, 'So I won't hang about for any tucker, as I'm off to throw a few shrimps on the barbie at home. Sorry your joey never turned up. G'day, everyone.'

Edgar and his nan goggled at me in speechless shock. I don't think tonight could have gone any worse.

8.03 p.m.
Texted Maddy that Edgar doesn't deserve to have any friends.

She texted back that everyone deserves to have friends.

Very annoyingly, she's right.

That's probably why his mum had tried to get that boy who collected rocks round.

I hope one day that rock-loving boy does pop up again.

And, yeah, I will admit that even Edgar needs a friend.

But that person could never be me.

8.22 p.m.
Tomorrow. Well, there's no bigger date in my calendar.

I'm back on Noah and Lily's vlog.

Chapter Six

Two Huge Surprises

Sunday March 2nd

2.36 p.m.
Mum drove me to Noah's house.

'How much longer,' she asked, 'do you think Noah and Lily will carry on making their vlogs?'

Mum made vlogging sound like a strange little hobby. Talk about patronising. So I began to explain about the global appeal of vlogs until she interrupted, 'When I was at school my best friend's dad used to make home movies. They were very good actually.'

But you couldn't compare home movies, for an audience of about four, to vlogs, which go around the world.

'Mum, Noah and Lily are huge international stars now.'

Mum shook her head in wonderment. 'I'm surprised you haven't all got bored of watching kids babbling away in their bedrooms by now.'

I swallowed very hard. I knew I shouldn't get annoyed by the way Mum was talking about this. It can't be easy being someone from the olden days. 'Mum, appearing on this vlog means everything to me.'

'Ha ha,' she laughed, as if I'd just said something hilarious. No doubt about it, she was getting weird again. I was sort of relieved she had some stuff to do, so couldn't come in and say 'Hello' to Noah and Lily.

3.35 p.m.
'Louis, welcome back to our vlogging family,' said Noah's mum, showing me into the kitchen. 'Noah and Lily won't be long, but they've had such a busy day, starting with a breakfast meeting with their manager about brand partnerships—'

'Wow, I'm impressed already,' I interrupted. 'A breakfast meeting. Not that I think anyone would like to watch me slurping my Coco Pops.'

She laughed. 'And three interviews later,

they've just squeezed in yet another one now. I say to them, "You must have one day away from it all," but they've just got so much to share. It never stops.'

Noah's mum was clearly well into all this. Why couldn't my mum be more like her? Perhaps Mum will be when *I* start having breakfast meetings.

'By the way,' she warned. 'Be prepared for a big shock when you see Noah.'

At last Noah and Lily bounded in. As usual, I blinked a lot when I first saw them. These two were properly famous after all. That's probably why they always seemed brighter and shinier than normal people. But then I noticed Noah had chopped off his big quiff.

It wasn't until I went upstairs to record the vlog though that I realised what a big deal his new haircut was. As usual, the webcam was balanced on a pile of books and it was easy to forget it was there, especially when Noah and Lily launched into one of their rows right away.

'I'm very angry with you, Noah. And so are all our followers, who have just one question for you – why did you do it?'

'My quiff was getting out of control,' he began.

'But you cut it without consulting our followers first,' Lily wailed. 'You do know you've totally ruined their week.' She started reading messages from deeply upset fans of Noah's quiff. 'You've given them such a horrible shock,' cried Lily, 'especially as it came right out of the blue. They had no chance to prepare themselves. So now you've got to wear *this*.' She flung a truly hideous, very cheap-looking black beret at him. At first I thought he was putting it on for a joke. But then Lily announced she'd designed it for him specially. And Noah, flashing a big smile, pointed helpfully at Lily's signature on the side.

Lily added reassuringly that there would be regular updates on Instagram as to how Noah's quiff was growing back. 'But now,' she cried, 'he's back. The boy to help you, whatever you're worried about. Louis the Laugh.'

I sat between them, not having a clue what any of the problems were going to be. They said it keeps everything fresher that way.

And we started with Greg, who really, really liked this girl in his class, but didn't think he was good-looking enough to ask her out. What should he do?

'Get a new head,' I grinned. 'No, first of all, Greg, take a look at me – diddy guy, with an onion-shaped face and ears like flying saucers.'

Lily went, 'Aaagh,' while Noah – disgustingly good looking, even in that beret – smirked away.

'But I've got the most sensational girlfriend called Maddy,' I continued. 'So if I can do it, you so can too. The thing is, Greg, we just have to work a bit harder – so be really interested in everything she says and ...'

After I'd finished helping Greg I answered four more problems, finishing up with Sarah who asked what she should do about her parents when they keep setting her goals.

'Stop them now, Sarah,' I said, 'because once parents begin doing this they can't stop. Soon they'll be giving you goals for cleaning your teeth and going to the loo.'

Noah started to laugh and I sped on.

'Sarah, tell your parents that if they even whisper the word "goal" in your presence again you will die. You will physically die, and—' But I had to stop then as Noah was laughing so much he'd fallen off his chair and was lying on the ground waving his legs in the air.

After we'd helped Noah up he patted me on the back and declared, 'Louis's advice always gets a ten out of ten from us. That's why, before he goes, we have a surprise for him.'

'I like surprises,' I grinned. 'I think ...'

'First of all, Louis, you know you are a total and complete nutcase,' said Lily. 'You even make Noah seem normal.'

'And that's not easy,' I laughed.

'And we never know what you're going to say next,' she said.

'Neither do I,' I quipped.

'And all the weeks you were away people kept asking us, "When's that hilarious little guy with the sticky-out ears coming back?"' Noah grinned at me. 'In fact, we've had such an epic response, we'd like you to be our one and only agony uncle and appear with us every single week. How does that sound to you, Louis the Laugh?'

I couldn't reply at first, as this was, without doubt, the greatest moment of my life. Or it would have been if Maddy had been here with me.

Then I spotted Noah and Lily watching me.

'You've made an incredibly wise decision,' I grinned. 'And it's the best news. The very best.'

4.50 p.m.
Mum was late coming back. It didn't matter. I called Maddy and she was practically levitating with excitement when she heard the news. She chatted for a bit with Noah and Lily too. And Noah described me to Maddy as his 'mischievous mate'. I was so proud. Then the doorbell rang. Guessing it was Mum, I sped to answer it. It was her, all right.

49

'Hey, Mum, I am the bearer of glad tidings.' And, as she stood on the doorstep, I blurted out my astonishing news. Now I was not expecting Mum to start breakdancing down the street. That's not her style. I'd have settled for her saying she was the proudest mum on this planet.

Instead she muttered, 'That's nice.' (Nice!) 'Now I'd love to meet Noah and Lily.' I took her into the kitchen. Noah's mum was there too. Mum shook hands and smiled at everyone, then stared again at Noah, who was still capering about in that odd-looking beret, before saying, 'Well, I don't need to ask if you've all been having fun.' She made it sound as if we were about three and had just been playing in the sandpit. Her patronising smile grew wider. 'And I'm sure Louis will be able to pop by and join in the fun again, say in a couple of months.'

If this moment had been filmed, within seconds Twitter would have been ablaze with people going **WHAT? WHAT JUST HAPPENED?** No wonder everyone's eyes were popping out of their heads. I was speechless with total shock.

'We went along with today as we'd promised, but from now on Louis is going to be far too busy to visit again for a while,' Mum continued.

'Busy appearing on other vlogs?' asked Lily at once.

'Of course not,' I replied quickly. 'This is the only vlog for me.'

Noah's mum got up and stood by my mum. 'I was exactly like you at the beginning,' Noah's mum said to her confidingly. 'Very sceptical.'

Mum's smile finally flickered.

'I thought vlogging was such a very odd thing to do,' Noah's mum went on. 'I still do, really. But you can't argue with success. And now they are doing so well I've had to give up my job as a nail technician to help them.'

'I bet you'd love to give up work too, wouldn't you, Mum?' I asked. 'Well, soon maybe you too—'

'So wonderful to have met you all,' interrupted Mum, 'and I look forward to seeing you all again – one day,' she added, before sweeping out.

I turned to Noah and Lily. 'Mum's so thrilled she's gone temporarily insane. But I'll be back next Sunday. You can count on it.'

5.56 p.m.

As you know, I don't often get really mad. But in the car I seethed and then seethed some more. I just couldn't stop.

'We're only calling a temporary halt to this vlogging, Louis,' Mum announced.

'But why are you doing it at all?' I demanded. That's when she said in a low, trembling voice, 'We know about you falling asleep in Mr Duncan's lesson.'

That gave me a jolt all right.

'Mum, it was a power— how do you know?'

'Mr Duncan told us.'

'No he didn't,' I declared. 'I was there with you at the parents' evening.'

'He rang me and your dad on Friday afternoon.'

'But Dunky had had his turn at the parents' evening. He can't call you as well. That's cheating.' I was outraged.

'Mr Duncan is very concerned about you, especially after you told him that since you started vlogging you can't sleep at night.'

'That's rubbish,' I replied.

'But it's exactly what you told Mr Duncan, isn't it, Louis? Tell the truth.'

I felt myself going red, right to my ears. 'No, well maybe – OK, yes, I probably did say something along those lines, but it isn't true.'

'Isn't it?'

'Of course not. Dunky's lessons are about as exciting as buying new socks. That's why I took forty winks. But I couldn't tell him that. You know how big-hearted I am.' But I could tell Mum didn't believe me. That's why I added in a low, urgent voice, 'Don't do it, Mum. Don't let Dunky's strange ideas get inside your head.'

Mum actually laughed.

'And don't ruin the biggest chance I've ever had.'

She stopped laughing. 'We've got your favourite meal waiting for you at home.'

'Why?' I demanded.

'So you realise that what we're going to do is not because you've done anything wrong.'

'And what are you going to do?' I asked.

'It's a surprise. For now,' said Mum.

An ice-cold shiver ran right through me.

Chapter Seven

In Deep Peril

6.25 p.m.

At home, wonderful smells greeted my nostrils. And Dad was setting up the table and placing crackers beside each plate, just as if it were Christmas. Elliot, the poor deluded turnip-head, was even getting excited. Especially when he saw Mum and Dad bringing in our favourite meals.

'We wanted to make tonight feel a bit special,' said Mum. 'So tuck in.'

Elliot spluttered something enthusiastic and totally unintelligible as bits of food sprayed out of his mouth.

'And we want you to realise that what we're

going to do is not in any way a punishment,' chipped in Dad.

'As it's our fault, of course, not yours,' said Mum.

Parents are at their most dangerous whenever they say that. No wonder I was finding it extremely hard to swallow.

'But there's no avoiding it. Your parents' evenings were ghastly,' said Mum.

'I warned you not to go,' I murmured. 'I told you no good can ever come from a parents' evening.'

'But if you've been half-hearted in your studies,' said Mum, 'it's because we've been half-hearted too.'

Dad agreed, nodding solemnly. 'We've been too busy with our own concerns – well, mine in particular – and we've neglected you both.'

'But I love you neglecting me,' I cried. 'In fact, I'd like much more of it.'

'All we want to do,' said Dad, 'is to open you up to new possibilities and make sure you are not limiting yourselves.'

I sighed heavily. 'What have you been reading on the internet now?'

Dad did look a bit embarrassed, but Mum pressed on. 'From tomorrow there are going to be some big changes in this house.'

Even Elliot stopped hurling food down his throat for a second. 'What kind of changes?' he quavered.

'All will be revealed tomorrow,' said Dad.

'But I can tell you,' Mum continued, 'that we're going to be much more involved in supporting you to meet the challenges of your schoolwork. There's no telling what we can achieve if we all pull together.'

Elliot and I could only gawp at her, our faces racked with horror. What on earth had Dunky said when he spoke to them on the phone?

'Now then,' asked Dad brightly, 'who'd like to pull a cracker?'

6.58 p.m.
In moments of deep peril – which this undoubtedly is – there's only one thing to do.

7.10 p.m.
Seconds after she received my text Maddy called.

'I've done everything to keep my parents happy,' I said. 'I even listened to ABBA with them.'

'You couldn't have done any more,' agreed Maddy.

'But still they've gone right back to their bad old ways. And I know they've been reading crazy stuff on the internet again.'

'That's modern parenting for you,' said Maddy. 'But nothing must stop you from becoming Noah and Lily's regular agony uncle, because I just know ...' She hesitated.

'Go on, Maddy.'

'That really is the breakthrough we've been waiting for.'

'And you are my agent. So you should know. But what do I do about my mum and dad?'

Maddy considered. 'Agree with them.'

'What!' I spluttered.

'Say they know best.'

'My mouth could never utter such words.'

'Try really hard, even say you'll do more homework. Get them thinking you agree with them – then ever so politely ask them to make one teeny exception.' Then she added, highly mysteriously, 'I'm sure this will work, but if it doesn't don't worry, just be sure and contact me right away.'

7.42 p.m.

I stood in front of Mum and Dad in the living room, with my feet slightly apart, as if I were going to sing a song. 'I've been thinking about what you've been saying about me trying harder with my schoolwork. And you know what, I will.

Who knows, I might even enjoy finding out about the rainfall in Canada.' This got no reaction at all from my parents. But then I thought of a good one. 'From now on, I won't munch a morsel of my tea until I've completed all my homework.'

'That sounds like an excellent idea—,' Dad began.

'Really?' Mum interrupted. 'I rather think it would be better for Louis to eat his tea first.'

'Well, whatever you think is best.' Undaunted, I continued, 'There's more. While I'm engaged in homework I could give up my phone to you, voluntarily.'

'That *is* an excellent idea,' Mum agreed.

'I'm full of them. So this means I shall be sitting at my desk, completely undisturbed and ready to focus all seven of my brain cells on stuff for school every single night. And I ask only one thing in return – let me go on Noah and Lily's vlog on Sundays as their resident agony uncle. And by the way, don't just think of me. Think of all those kids in the world who are waiting for my advice.'

If I say so myself, it was an incredibly stirring speech.

I waited for Mum and Dad to spring up and declare, 'Now you've explained it so clearly we realise we couldn't possibly stand in your way.

Forgive us, Louis, for our foolish behaviour.'
(And, of course, I would, because I'm great like
that.)

Instead, neither of them said a word. Dad
stared down at his hands, even turning them
over a few times, while Mum continued to survey
the wall over my head. 'We do know what this
means to you,' croaked Dad at last.

'And not just me,' I replied. 'Don't forget all
those kids around the world.'

'But Louis, you fell asleep in the middle of a
lesson,' said Mum.

'A power nap,' I corrected warily.

'And your teacher believes that you're
allowing a hobby,' said Mum, 'to distract you
from all your lessons.'

'Mum, I explained that—'

'We have to get you back on track,' she said.

'But I'm on track now! Or at least I was until
you messed everything up.'

'Look, we'll make a deal with you,' said Dad.
'If you give our new approach a chance, you
can return to your vlogging in just two months.
And you can keep your phone, but only until
bedtime. We want you to be getting a proper
night's sleep so you're not too tired to do your
schoolwork. How about that?'

'Two months!' I echoed disbelievingly. 'I can't

hang about all that time while my life slips by. I have to start this Sunday otherwise ... well, there are tons of people ready to jump into my shoes ... so Noah and Lily will just use one of them.'

'Well, I'm sure there'll be something else,' said Mum breezily. 'Something even more fun.'

'Not a chance like this,' I exclaimed. 'Believe me.'

But Mum and Dad just smiled, totally unconcerned. This is what happens when parents don't understand modern life today.

There was only one thing I could do now. So I called Maddy back.

And soon she was telling me something truly amazing. Something which every kid should know.

How to fool your parents into doing whatever you want.

Chapter Eight

How to Fool Your Parents

8.10 p.m.
Maddy said there is one practically foolproof way to fool your parents. You have to be extremely careful not to over-use it though. That is why she has never told me about it before. It must be saved for total and complete emergencies.

Like this.

And all I've got to do is utter fourteen words.

Fourteen *magic* words.

Maddy suggested I practise how I say them too. So, for a start, I have to make sure I get the right expression on my face (dead sincere).

61

I mustn't rush the words either as that dilutes their extraordinary power.

She also advised I speak from my stomach. This makes my voice deeper, which somehow adds to the words' impact. So over and over in my bedroom I repeated those words – in my deepest voice.

Now at last I'm ready to unleash them.

Let the magic begin.

8.35 p.m.

Bounced into the kitchen where Mum and Dad eyed me a bit warily, I thought. They were expecting another argument. 'Can I ask you something?' I began.

'Yes,' said Mum cautiously, before adding, 'Louis, are you getting a cold?'

'Oh no,' I assured her. I'd already started practising my deep voice. Then I growled from my stomach the magic fourteen words: 'Who are the very best parents in the world? You are. Yes, you are.'

And instantly something brilliant happened. My parents' faces just transformed. They looked ten years younger for a start. No, they truly did. And their faces were taken over by the widest happiest smiles you've ever seen.

'What a lovely thing to say,' cried Mum softly.

And then they both started hugging me.

Maddy certainly didn't underestimate the power of those words. And every kid should know them. In fact, I'd put this on the school syllabus. A stupendously simple way to fool your parents – I tell you, no one would want to miss the class when they taught that.

Dad, still deeply moved, murmured, 'It's a long time since you said anything like that, Louis.'

'In fact, I don't remember you ever saying it,' cried Mum.

'Doesn't mean I wasn't thinking it though,' I said. 'And now I've come right out and said it.'

'It means a lot,' said Dad.

'I'm sure,' I agreed.

And both Mum and Dad were glowing. There's no other word for it.

'Especially now,' added Dad.

'Oh really,' I said politely.

'Yes, because it must mean you agree with us,' said Dad.

'Well, er ...' I began.

'You realise that schoolwork is not an optional extra,' said Mum. 'And you must give it your very best effort.'

'Totally on board for that, Mum,' I assured her.

They both beamed at me.

'Only you will let me appear on Noah and Lily's vlog on Sundays, won't you?' The words came out in a rush. And I forgot to talk from my stomach.

And my parents weren't beaming at me any more either. Instead they looked, well, disillusioned would be the best way to describe it.

'All those nice things you said about us being the best parents were just to butter us up,' sighed Mum.

'You didn't actually mean a word of it,' said Dad, not looking even ten seconds younger any more.

'You are such cynics,' I cried. 'Of course I meant it. But ... about Sunday?'

'Sorry, Louis,' said Mum flatly. 'No deal.'

8.45 p.m.

Maddy texted that this scheme was **PRACTICALLY FOOLPROOF**. It had let her down only once, when she tried to persuade her parents to allow her to stay in the UK while they skipped off to America.

And whenever those magic words fail it means but one thing.

Your parents must be under a very heavy spell indeed.

So it won't be easy, but I'll never give up.

Chapter Nine

Extremely Noisy

Monday March 3rd

4.50 p.m.
My ears have just been assaulted.

Arrived home to be greeted by an ear-splitting racket. A high-pitched, very screechy racket — like a never-ending train whistle.

I followed the din into the living room where Dad and Elliot were both playing recorders. Dad's was old and wooden, while Elliot's was cheaper-looking and a grubby white colour. It was hard to tell who was more out of tune.

They stopped when they saw me. 'Just warming up,' cried Dad, 'and getting our lips moving. Don't worry, Louis, your recorder is on its way.'

'That's really cheered me up,' I replied with undisguised sarcasm.

'Your mum is buying it right now, in fact,' Dad continued. 'It's only for you to learn on. Then later we'll get you a proper one to—'

'Dad, I'm not learning the recorder,' I declared, folding my arms.

'That's where you are wrong,' said Dad. 'We're all learning the recorder together, your mum and me too. I thought it would be something easy to start with, before we move on to the violin.'

'What!' I exclaimed.

'I know all about the recorder,' explained Dad. 'I used to play in the school recorder club every Wednesday lunch time.' Far-off memories were clearly stirring inside him as he smiled nostalgically.

'Here, you have a go,' said Elliot, throwing his bargain-basement recorder at me.

Dad started fussing about, telling me where I should put my thumbs. Then, very half-heartedly, I blew into it, releasing this high-pitched shriek which sounded exactly like a banshee on an off day. Then I exclaimed disgustedly, 'Ugh! I can taste spit.'

'Ha ha!' yelled Elliot, jumping about delightedly. 'You fell for it. That was all my spit too ...'

'Why, you—' I began and started flicking the recorder at him, showering him in spittle.

'Ew!' screeched Elliot. 'I felt that.'

'All right, boys, calm down,' interrupted Dad. 'We are going to do this right. Now before you can play you need to learn how to breathe properly. So I want you both to watch me very closely. See how I'm taking a very deep breath? And now another one ...' That's when Dad started to cough. Soon his coughing grew louder and faster.

'Hey, Dad, you sound better than the recorder,' I quipped. 'Definitely more in tune.'

But Dad didn't answer. He couldn't – he was too busy coughing. Growing alarmed now, I tore off to get him some water.

'Hurry up!' yelled Elliot. 'Dad's face is turning red. I think he's about to explode.'

I rushed back. Dad snatched the glass from me, managing to spill more than half the water all over himself. But after he'd had a few gulps he started to breathe more naturally. 'Take some deep breaths,' I urged.

'I'm all right,' he gasped.

'You need to sit down though,' I said.

Elliot and I were helping him into a chair when Mum came back.

'Whatever's happened?' she began.

'It's all right, Mum,' I explained. 'Dad just injured himself breathing, that's all.'

6.30 p.m.

Mum and Dad just popped their heads round my bedroom door. 'Don't worry,' said Mum. 'We shan't sit and watch you do your homework.'

They had actually done that before. I remember Dad lolling about on my bed slurping peppermints for hours. And it was so tiring having to pretend I was working all that time.

'We'll go now and let you get stuck in,' said Dad.

So that's exactly what I did – on my very own comedy homework. Five minutes on my history homework, then I wrote down forty new jokes. Where humour is concerned I'm a definite over-achiever.

7.22 p.m.

Just packing away when I noticed my bedroom was swarming with parents again. 'How did you get on?' asked Dad eagerly.

'Really well, Dad. I'm a bit shattered now though, what with doing all that homework and saving your life earlier.'

Quite unimpressed by my heroism they asked

if they could see my homework.

'Oh, it's some rhubarb about the changing role of Parliament since Tudor times. You wouldn't want to clutter up your brain reading that.'

And normally they wouldn't. But they aren't themselves right now and they practically demanded I show it to them. They read it together, saying a few bits aloud in really shocked tones.

'It hasn't got to be in until Wednesday, so I might add a bit more to it later,' I explained airily, 'or I might not.'

'Louis, this essay is our fault,' said Mum.

'If you say so.' Humour them, Maddy had said.

'We haven't provided the right environment for you to learn and challenge yourself,' said Dad.

'I wouldn't worry about it,' I grinned cheerfully at them.

'The thing is, Louis,' said Mum, staring sternly down at my history essay. 'Being good at anything requires effort.'

'But what if you'll never be any good at something?' I asked. 'Surely it's much better to spend your time on what you *are* good at – like being on a world-famous vlog.'

Mum sighed heavily. 'Louis, you're just not living in the real world.' And do you know, she

69

said that as if it was a bad thing.

Then Dad chipped in. 'I'll tell you something, Louis, when I started playing the recorder again today I was disappointed. I thought I'd sound much better than that. But am I going to give up?'

'Oh, yes please,' I muttered.

'No way,' cried Dad. 'I'm just going to put in even more effort. Has that inspired you at all?'

'No,' I replied.

'And we're going to help you with your homework,' said Mum. 'Not by writing it for you—' (That was the only help I was interested in.) '—but by giving you more stimulation,' continued Mum. 'I'll bring in some books you can study.'

'And I,' said Dad, 'will supply you with everything I can find on the internet.'

'I really don't like to put you to all this trouble,' I said.

'As we said to Elliot a few minutes ago,' cried Mum, 'we are raising the bar much higher for you both. Something we should have done a long time ago. I'm just so sorry we didn't do it before.'

The more your parents apologise to you, the madder and more crazy and unreasonable they are. A true Louis fact.

7.50 p.m.
Mum has hurled a pile of books in my direction. And Dad has just carried in eight zillion pieces of paper he's printed off. As he was leaning on my desk he farted. Very loudly! That was undoubtedly the highlight of my entire evening.

Tuesday March 4th

5.10 p.m.
All four of us played 'Frère Jacques' tonight – not that you could tell what it was. 'Is your recorder talking to you yet?' Dad asked me.

'Oh yeah,' I replied. 'It's saying, leave me alone.'

Then Mum said she and Dad are really looking forward to seeing my history essay. Actually they'll find it remarkably unchanged from yesterday. Do you think they'll notice?

7.05 p.m.
Mum and Dad have just read my history essay again. And I really thought Dad was going to cry. 'This isn't any better than your last effort,' he spluttered. (Actually it *was* my last effort.)

Then they babbled something about me digging deeper.

'Louis, we're just not accepting work of that

standard from you,' said Dad.

They're coming back at half past eight.

7.52 p.m.
I really have tried reading this guff Dad ran off for me, but none of it makes any sense to me.

It's hopeless.

7.55 p.m.
My parents will keep on at me until this essay improves. And anyway I've got to keep in with them so they somehow change their minds about Sunday. I will put up with anything if it means I can appear on Noah and Lily's vlog.

But I really have to draw the line at doing homework.

7.56 p.m.
If only Maddy was here.

7.57 p.m.
There's no one else. Well, I suppose there is actually. One person.

7.58 p.m.
And I'm so totally desperate. I'm going to close my bedroom door extremely tightly and call him now.

Chapter Ten

My Parents Turn into Supervillains

8.15 p.m.

Edgar sounded extremely cross. 'I have nothing to say to you.'

'That's excellent news and you can ring off the very second after you've done me a favour. I want you to tell me everything you know about the changing role of Parliament during the time of the Tudors.'

'What, *now*?' asked Edgar.

'Of course now – and talk fast. And try and make it sound intellectual ...'

'Actually I am an intellectual,' said Edgar.

'Away you go then,' I said.

I scribbled furiously while Edgar speed-talked about Henry VIII and the dissolution of the monasteries and ... but why should I bore you with it too? It made my head ache just writing it all down.

Finally he said, 'And that's everything I know,' and rang off before I could even thank him.

8.40 p.m.
Mum and Dad have just read my new history essay.

'Now the handwriting could be better,' began Mum. 'But, Louis' – a gleam actually came in her eyes – 'the content is absolutely superb.'

'Yes, well done, Louis.' That gleam was in Dad's eyes too. But then this is what they'd always dreamed of – a super swot for a son. 'We knew you'd find a way to rewrite this essay,' went on Dad.

'Oh yes, I found a way,' I agreed.

'And I think we're finally seeing what you're capable of,' Dad went on.

Again I agreed. Who'd have thought I was capable of asking Edgar – of all people – for a favour?

Wednesday March 5th

3.00 p.m.
A new boy called Jack has joined our school. Mrs Hare asked if anyone would like to look after him. Not one person volunteered. I know – what a friendly place. So finally I said I would.

As Jack and I were leaving I felt a hand on my shoulder. 'It's super that you want to help,' cooed Mrs Hare. 'But we don't want Jack doing anything stupid, do we, Louis?'

'Got any suggestions?' I asked.

How did I get such a bad rep?

I'm almost hurt.

4.35 p.m.
I ABSOLUTELY HATE, LOATHE AND DE-TEST having to play that cheap little recorder. I think I'd probably rather be in detention. In fact, I know I would. At least it would be peaceful.

When I got home Dad and Elliot had already started playing something (Mum was still at work or so she was pretending) and I tell you, it made an electric drill sound tuneful.

Then I was forced to join in because it's so important we make a racket as a family. Afterwards Dad was saying, 'I think you're both letting in too much air.'

'Or maybe,' I said, 'Elliot and I are just rubbish at blowing the recorder.'

Dad shook his head at me. 'A bad attitude gets you nowhere. Now, do you know what I was doing before you came home?'

'Buying some ear plugs?' I suggested.

'I've been practising and practising a tune I know you will recognise. So come on, let me inspire you to try harder. Just listen to this.'

Dad was off then with this rapt expression on his face, while he blasted out something truly ear-splitting. Elliot looked at me as if to say *the things parents put us through*. At the end Dad asked eagerly, 'So, boys, what was that?'

'Not a clue,' said Elliot.

'Come on, you must have recognized that, Louis.'

'No, but a cat has started wailing outside in sympathy.'

'It was the theme tune from *The Simpsons*,' said Dad.

'Really?' I exclaimed in total amazement.

'Yes.' Dad shook his head at me again. 'I'm very surprised you didn't recognise it, as it is one of your favourite shows.'

'Dad, me blowing my nose sounds more like *The Simpsons* than that.' Then he looked so crestfallen I had to add, 'Good try though. Now, can we rest our ears for several centuries?'

6.55 p.m.
My parents' faces crumpled with disappointment when they saw my geography and English homework.

'We know you can do better,' said Mum. 'Just dig deep again, like you did last night.'

'I will need to have complete silence and not be disturbed,' I said.

'We understand,' said Dad. They actually tiptoed out. I closed the door tightly and rang Edgar again.

7.31 p.m.
It was just like turning on a tap. I only had to say a subject and Edgar was gabbling away. And it all sounded mega impressive. In other words, I didn't understand any of it.

I must admit I was dead grateful to Edgar. 'If I had any spare cash or gift tokens or lucky heather I'd drop them round to you now. Your brain should be left to science—'

'Actually none of those questions were the least bit difficult,' he interrupted.

I immediately stopped feeling grateful to him after that.

7.50 p.m.

Mum and Dad knocked on my door and then came in, almost shyly.

'So how are you getting on?' asked Mum.

'Just finished them both.' I sat back in my chair with a little sigh.

'May we have a peek?' Mum had picked up my English essay before I could reply, while Dad was perusing my geography offering in a dazed sort of way.

And soon Mum was cooing, 'Louis, this is really very good.'

'So is this,' said Dad. 'If only we'd seen work of this standard from you before.'

I nodded. I should have thought of Edgar doing my homework ages ago.

'We're so proud of you,' said Mum.

I couldn't help showing off a bit. 'Well, once I started, I couldn't write quickly enough.' That was sort of true. Edgar spoke really fast.

'This is a real breakthrough.' Mum was bursting with joy now.

I'd totally fooled them *and* made them really happy, so that everyone was a winner.

And so it was the perfect moment to ask ...

'As a reward for all my hard labour, can I appear on Noah and Lily's vlog this Sunday? Please.'

A guarded look immediately appeared on both their faces. 'Go on,' I urged. 'I have done stupendous homework for a record-breaking two nights.'

Mum and Dad exchanged glances before Mum said quite gently, 'Sorry, love, but you're not ready yet.'

'Mum, I so am.'

'When you put *all* your energy into your schoolwork, just look at what you can achieve!' Mum argued.

'So keep following our regime for now,' added Dad. 'But, as promised, in a couple of months ...'

I was livid. I'd put up with playing the recorder and being imprisoned in my bedroom doing homework in the hope they'd see sense. But they were still being totally unreasonable. That's why I burst out, 'Actually I didn't write a single word of any of those essays. Edgar did it all.'

'Edgar!' cried Dad. 'But he hasn't even been here.'

'I communicated with him on this handy new invention called the mobile phone, into which he kindly rattled off all the stuff I wrote in my essays, as he's highly intelligent. In fact, he's probably curled up with a book of quadratic equations right now. Your perfect son, in fact.'

Yes, I'd totally ruined the party atmosphere. But they'd brought it on themselves, hadn't they?

'We're very disappointed in you,' said Mum and Dad together.

'And I'm very disappointed in you,' I replied. After they'd left the room. And very quietly.

I meant it though.

8.00 p.m.

I immediately rang Maddy. She, of course, was still marooned at school, though luckily it was the start of lunch time there.

'I know, I shouldn't have got mad at them,' I said.

'What else can you do,' she replied, 'when your parents start turning into supervillains?'

Maddy always puts things so brilliantly.

'The only time I get any peace from them I'm in bed.'

'It must be so grim.'

'And I can't tell them how hopelessly wrong they are as they never listen to me. Not properly anyhow. All they can think about are their hopes for me. I want to somehow wake them up by doing something so crazy—'

'Louis, I think I've got it,' she interrupted excitedly.

I was beyond impressed. To come up with a plan at such speed and when she's zillions of miles away too.

'I've thought of a way to get their attention, all right. But it won't be easy.'

Then Maddy told me what it was.

It was dead clever, all right.

But could even I actually do that?

Chapter Eleven
The PJ Protest

8.13 p.m.
No, I couldn't.

Too crazy, too embarrassing – even for a total show-off like me.

8.21 p.m.
I might have talked myself out of Maddy's idea if Poppy hadn't rung.

'Why didn't you tell me?' Poppy demanded at once.

'Tell you what?'

'That you are going to be on Noah and Lily's vlog every single week. I mean, that's sensational news and you didn't say a word to me about it.'

'Ah, but Poppy,' I said quickly, 'you are forgetting something. I'm now too important and famous to talk to you myself these days. But I asked my butler, Fortescue, to inform you.'

'Well, he didn't, and I've just caught up with you on last Sunday's show. You were brilliantly funny, of course. And I am so happy for you, Louis. You really deserve this break.'

'That is true.'

She laughed again. 'I bet you're over the moon.'

'I'll check with Fortescue.'

All week people at school have asked me about being Noah and Lily's regular agony uncle. I didn't want them to know all my dreams had coming crashing round my ears, as most of them would gloat over such catastrophic news. So I merely grinned away and said how excited I was.

But Poppy was totally different. She'd be genuinely upset for me. I couldn't admit the truth even to her. I just didn't want to say the words aloud, as that would mean admitting I really had lost my big chance, which I almost certainly had. Unless ... that's when Maddy's plan popped into my head again.

Meanwhile, Poppy was saying, 'I've got a bit of news too. You know that new variety show on television every Sunday?'

'You're not going to be on it?' I interrupted.

'I am. And it's live as well.'

'Wow, Poppy,' was all I managed to say. Well, it's hard to speak when you're grinding your teeth with jealousy. But it passed in a flash.

No, it really did, as Poppy is amazing. You should see her whizzing round that stage in her wheelchair performing four magic tricks at once. She's worked so incredibly hard too. Her grandad – who is also a magician – taught her everything she knows. But even he admits she's better than him now.

Plus, she's an incredible friend. We met on a TV talent show, which she won. Her prize was to have her own half-hour satellite show. And who did she pick to appear on it with her?

Me.

So I could say, quite genuinely, 'I'm dead chuffed for you, Poppy.'

'Let's watch each other,' she said, 'and then give our genuine opinions.'

'It's a deal,' I said.

The moment Poppy rang off I reached a major decision.

Right now, nothing I can say reaches my mum and dad.

But Maddy's idea is so mad and different

it might just bring them to their senses. And surely it's worth trying anything, however daft, if it means I get onto that vlog. So why on earth am I hesitating?

Haven't a clue.

8.30 p.m.
I wanted to see if I could get Elliot to join me in my plan tomorrow. He was already in bed with his light off. But I whispered to him what my scheme was.

That made him leap up in bed, all right.

But he didn't need as much persuading as I'd expected. He's more fed-up with what's happening in this house than I'd realised.

And so both Elliot and I will be protesting together tomorrow.

Thursday March 6th

7.18 a.m.
Mum has just dropped in to check if I'm awake. She hasn't a clue what is about to happen. And I don't feel as nervous as I'd expected I would. Now I just want to get on with it.

7.31 a.m.
Took off my old pyjamas and then dug out my

best ones – the blue stripey ones. They seemed to smile up at me in a friendly, welcoming way as if delighted to be a big part of this. These pyjamas have a good collar and pockets and look really smart, I thought, as I stared at myself in them. Then I put on my school tie and finally I added my blazer. No one can say I'm not in uniform.

Now I look – well, incredibly weird actually. But right now I don't care. In fact, I'm enjoying myself.

7.38 a.m.
I wandered into Elliot's room. He was also wearing his school blazer over his admittedly far less impressive jim-jams. He grinned nervously at me. 'Are we actually going to do this?'

'Of course. In fact, I feel so relaxed in these pyjamas. I wouldn't be surprised if you and I start a trend. Soon I bet pupils will be arriving at school all over the country dressed like this.'

'But what will Mum and Dad say?' asked Elliot, sounding scared and excited at the same time.

'We'll soon find out,' I said.

7.58 a.m.
'At last,' sighed Mum, without properly turning

round to look at Elliot and me. 'I've got to leave a bit earlier this morning, but Dad's working at home today so ...' Her voice fell away as she finally saw us. She then opened and closed her mouth twice, like a very stunned goldfish.

Elliot giggled nervously.

'But ... but ...' she struggled for words as we sat down at the kitchen table. 'Why on earth are you both still in your pyjamas?'

'I had a feeling you might ask us that—' I began.

'Go upstairs and get changed at once!' she ordered.

That was a voice you don't argue with. Elliot had even started to get up until he looked at me and promptly sat down again, his head lowered.

'I'm sorry, Mum, we can't do that,' I said. 'This is an official PJ protest. We will, in fact, be attending school like this unless you and Dad actually listen to what we have to say. It's up to you.'

'We haven't got time for this now, boys!' But her voice had gone a tiny bit croaky. This gave me confidence.

'Since Monday,' I said, 'Elliot and I have been a persecuted minority. Persecuted by you and Dad.'

'We really have,' agreed Elliot through a

mouthful of toast.

'The only time you give us any peace is when we're in our pyjamas,' I said. 'That is why we will keep them on today.'

Then Dad appeared.

'They claim they're are going to school like this,' said Mum.

'You've got to admit, Dad, it's a good look,' I declared, with a little smile.

He gave a short laugh. 'All right, boys, you've brightened up the morning. Time to put on your proper school uniform now.'

'When you and Mum change your ways and listen to us and our concerns, then we will suspend this action.' I looked at him hopefully.

Dad stared at us for a moment. I could almost hear him thinking, OK, boys, go to school in your pyjamas. Mum looked nearly as startled as we did. But I heard Dad whisper to her in the kitchen, 'They won't even go outside like that.'

8.18 a.m.
'I hope you are upstairs getting changed,' calls Mum.

'The joke's definitely over now,' shouts Dad.

Elliot is leaping about in my bedroom.

'This is excellent fun,' he laughs.

8.30 a.m.

Elliot and I bounce downstairs.

'Here they come,' hisses Mum.

'Let's not say anything more about it,' says Dad. 'They've had their little protest and got it out of their system.'

They are completely confident that we will be in our normal drab uniform again.

Then they see us. They are both stunned. Elliot can't stop giggling.

'Bye then,' I say.

That's when a voice quavers behind me. 'But we're not really going to do this, are we?'

'Oh yes,' I reply briskly.

'We're *actually* going to school like this?' asks Elliot. Then he freezes. 'Louis, I can't,' he squeaks. 'Sorry.'

And he looks so gutted I say to him, 'Don't worry about it. You've done incredibly well.'

His face actually glows with pride for a moment before he scurries back upstairs.

'Now hurry up,' Mum calls after him, before adding, 'both of you.'

While Dad says confidently, 'You can leave it to me now.'

'Well, if you're sure,' replies Mum. 'I am late already.'

They really think it's all over, so I slip upstairs

after Elliot. And the moment Mum drives off, I stroll downstairs again.

Dad groans. 'A joke is a joke.'

'Dad, this – and I speak as a comedian – is no joke. But you can stop me. Just say you'll listen to us. Well, me really. That's all I ask.'

Dad actually hesitates, but then he spots Elliot, halfway down the stairs now, in his school trousers but still wearing a pyjama top.

'No, I won't be held to ransom like this. This is not the way we communicate in our family.'

'I bid you good day then,' I say. I bend down, put on my shoes and stride purposely towards the front door. Then I stop and announce, 'It doesn't look very cold out this morning, which is handy.'

Yes, I'm playing for time.

The very last thing I want is to parade outside in my PJs. But I mustn't let Dad see that.

This really is a giant game of bluff.

Next I open the front door. 'Yeah, it's quite mild outside,' I declare breezily. 'Perfect weather, in fact, for an early morning stroll in my PJs.'

Not a word from Dad.

'Bye then, again,' I call.

Then a few seconds later. 'Really bye this time.'

And a few seconds after that. 'I'M ACTUALLY

GOING NOW – IN MY PYJAMAS.'

I'm still hovering on the doorstep when Dad's phone rings and I hear him say, 'Thanks for calling, Giles. I wanted to ask you ...'

But I don't see Elliot dart downstairs and shut the front door, he moves so fast. I just hear the door slam deafeningly.

Then Elliot yells through the letterbox. 'Off you go then.'

What on earth do I do now?

Chapter Twelve

The New School Uniform

Got two choices really.

I either ring on the front door and skulk back inside.

Or, or – I wander the streets in my night attire.

'Chicken, chicken,' yells Elliot (more than somewhat hypocritically) through the letterbox.

That's when, and feeling exactly as if I'm in a dream, I give him a cheery wave and breeze out of our drive and up the road. I won't get very far. Dad will come off the phone soon and immediately tear after me.

I'm spotted right away. The two little boys –
even tinier than Elliot – are getting into their
car when they stop, point at me and roar with
laughter.

'Louis has still got his jimmy jams on,' they
shout.

Their mum then notices too and smiles at
me in a dazed sort of way. 'H-e-l-l-o,' she says,
gawping.

'Hiya, nice day,' I say nonchalantly.

She calls after me, 'Is this for a television
show?'

'Probably,' I call back.

I stroll on, passing next a girl from my school
who does a massive double take. 'Louis, you do
know you've still got your pyjamas on.'

'Don't be silly,' I say, 'this is the new school
uniform.'

'Wh-aat!'

'Yeah, the brand new look, which I am trying
out today. So what do you think?'

'Wh-aat?' she says again.

'It's dead comfortable and great if you want to
do a spot of karate,' I continue, 'so I'm definitely
going to recommend it.'

'You're going to sit in lessons like that?' she
shouted.

'Of course, and soon everyone will be dressing

like this too. But you saw it first.'

And I stroll past her without a quiver.

No one would guess that one question is nagging away at me.

Am I really going to rock into school in my pyjamas?

8.45 a.m.
I'd just left my road when a girl in my year sees me and laughs and laughs. 'You're so mad,' she cries. 'Can I have a picture?'

'Of course,' I reply. While she's snapping away a car pulls up alongside us. 'Get in, Louis,' urges Dad hoarsely.

'Very kind of you,' I reply, 'but I'm so enjoying the walk. Unless you are prepared to listen to my—'

'Just get in!' roars Dad.

But I merely give him a jaunty wave. I'm not giving in now. Then I think Dad is honking me. But instead it's two guys in a van who yell out, 'Hey, sleeping beauty!'

I grin back at them, while quickening my pace. By the time I reach the school gates I've posed for three more pics and have gathered a gaggle of pupils behind me, while drivers slow down their cars to gawp at me in total amazement.

And one car actually follows me through the

school gates – even though it's strictly forbidden for parents to do this. 'Louis!' screeches Dad at me through the window. 'Listen to me, we understand your concerns and realise we've got to respond to them.'

I whirl round, relief flooding in through me. At last. To be honest, I hadn't been looking forward to appearing in lessons dressed like this. 'We'll have a family meeting tonight, I promise. Now get in the car,' urges Dad. 'And come home and get changed.'

My mission complete, I can do exactly that.

Only that's when I hear my name being hissed. A clearly agitated Dunky comes floating towards me.

Trust him to be on duty today.

He points at me, while swelling like a balloon. 'What is the meaning of this extraordinary garb?' he splutters as the crowd around me grows even larger.

I stagger back from him. 'What ... am I doing here?' Then I turned huge, bewildered eyes at him. 'I'm so confused ... I was in my bed, all snug and cosy and fast asleep and the next thing I know, I'm here. I really think I must have sleep-walked all the way to school, sir.' Before Dunky can reply, I call out, 'Thank goodness, there's my dad, come to take me home.' Then I fall into Dad's car, which takes off at a speed any getaway vehicle would envy.

9.15 a.m.
Yeah, I'm back at school. And in my regular dreary uniform.

Do you know what I think? Once a week everyone should be allowed to come to school in their pyjamas – teachers as well. For a start, everyone would be much more relaxed. So it would totally improve the atmosphere (which, let's face it, could do with improving).

Pictures of me in my night attire seem to be popping up everywhere and Dunky wants to see me at break time. I don't think it's to ask me where I got my pyjamas.

But none of that matters at all. What's important is that my pyjama protest actually worked.

I've done it!

4.32 p.m.
Spoiler alert.

No, I haven't.

For once I was actually looking forward to a family meeting. Well, who wouldn't enjoy hearing their parents apologising to them?

I decided they needn't suffer too much. Once

they'd admitted the error of their ways and promised on a stack of joke books never to stop me appearing on Noah and Lily's vlog again for the whole of their lives, I'd let the matter drop.

'We have been listening carefully to what you have both told us,' Mum began.

'But I haven't told you anything,' interrupted Elliot.

'We told them plenty when we put our pyjamas on to go to school,' I muttered.

'And we agree with you,' Mum went on. 'We have put too much pressure on you regarding your homework. From now on we will only suggest how you could improve your homework. Suggestions we hope you will follow, but the final decision must be yours, not ours.'

'And Louis, if you want to get some help from your friend Edgar, that's fine too.' Dad was grinning at me now. 'We like him actually.'

This only shows what terrible taste my parents have.

'Helping doesn't mean Edgar writes the whole thing for you, though,' Mum had to cut in.

'But sometimes it can be easier to ask for assistance from someone your own age, not old relics like us. We must realise that now and we should have seen it before.' Dad looked at Elliot and me as if he'd said something highly significant. But none of this had me leaping about. I thought the best was still to come.

Only it wasn't.

Mum and Dad stopped there. Then Dad asked if there were any questions.

'Can we chuck those lousy recorders away now?' asked Elliot.

Dad looked shocked. 'But this is our family challenge! And we're going to learn "Three Blind Mice" tomorrow.'

Elliot gulped in horror.

Then I asked my question. 'What about Sunday, and Noah and Lily's vlog?' I waited, holding my breath.

Mum and Dad shifted about awkwardly. There was a tiny pause. 'For now,' said Dad quietly, 'the ban still stands. Of course, in the—'

'Then you got me out of my pyjamas under false pretences,' I cried angrily.

'It's the part of being a parent I like least,' sighed Dad, 'having to say no. But we have compromised. And you must too.'

'We just want to ensure you have the time and space to really achieve,' chipped in Mum.

'But I will be really achieving on Sunday,' I said. They totally ignored this (parents are brilliant at not hearing things when they don't want to).

98

'Now, is there anything else either of you would like to say?' asked Dad.

Here's what I wanted to say: 'I know you're my mum and dad. But there are times when I wish you were in a galaxy far, far away. And this is definitely one of those times.'

But what would be the point? Maddy was right, whatever sort of parenting spell they were under was so powerful, it was unbreakable right now.

So then Dad rubbed his hands and declared, 'Well, I think this has all been extremely helpful.'

He didn't even seem to notice how Elliot's and my face had dropped to the ground – or see how wearily we trudged upstairs.

9.05 p.m.
Just before my phone was taken away for the night I had a brief but brilliant convo with Maddy.

She said, 'OK, your mum and dad can't be brought to their senses. But we fight on.'

'Great. How?'

'You'll just have to escape on Sunday and go and do the vlog without them realising.'

'That could be extremely hairy,' I said.

'But you can do it,' said Maddy, 'with a bit of help from me.'

Now I feel ashamed for getting so down-hearted.

Maddy is so right.

I'm not beaten yet.

Chapter Thirteen

The Great Escape

Friday March 7th

8.07 a.m.
Maddy texted me. I must stay under the radar and not give my parents the tiniest hint that I am planning a break for freedom this Sunday.

But how can I just disappear for long enough to get to Noah and Lily's and back, *and* do the vlog, without arousing their suspicions? Maddy says she is working on that one.

8.09 a.m.
At breakfast my parents are super smiley. I'm sure they think they've won.

4.25 p.m.
'Three Blind Mice' is, without doubt, the worst song in the world. But when played loudly and completely out of tune it is beyond horrific. Sweat formed on Dad's forehead as he kept attempting to get us all to play in harmony. In the end Elliot yelled, 'My ears will drop off if I have to listen to it any more.'

Long after we'd stopped, the room was still vibrating.

7.40 p.m.
Just had a top-secret conversation with Maddy who (yes, you guessed it) is still at school.

Here's her plan of campaign for Sunday:

In the afternoon I tell my parents I'm going round to Edgar's house.

I instantly objected but then stopped. Actually it was a good idea, especially as my parents like him and somehow believe we're buddies. I suggested I tell them Edgar is going to help me with my homework. (So I must remember to take some school books with me.)

Next, I actually do go to Edgar's house. A taxi will be waiting there to whiz me to Noah's place.

'The only thing is,' I paused in some embarrassment, 'I'm not sure I'll have enough cash ...'

'Don't worry, Edgar will lend you the rest,' said Maddy.

'Really!' I was stunned.

'He appreciates that this is a total emergency,' went on Maddy.

We worked out that the journey to Noah and Lily's house will take about twenty minutes. Recording the vlog will take another forty-five minutes tops, then it'll be another twenty minutes returning to Edgar's home. So I could be back at my house again in less than two hours without my parents suspecting a thing.

Saturday March 8th

5.02 p.m.

Mum and Dad are totally fine about me popping round to Edgar's tomorrow.

Dad even asked, 'Does Edgar play any musical instruments?'

'Knowing him I'd say yes,' I began.

'Well, maybe he could pop round one day and inspire us all,' suggested Dad brightly.

'Maybe,' I said faintly.

'I'm so glad you are spending some time with Edgar tomorrow,' said Mum.

Yes, all of about twenty seconds when he — very generously, I must admit — tops up my money to pay the taxi fare.

'He's someone worth making the effort to get to know,' went on Mum. 'Well done, Louis.'

So finally – after many attempts – I've managed to fool them. My parents actually believe I've given up on the biggest chance of my life to instead do homework with Edgar.

I suppose the thing is they'd really like that to be true. I guess I can fool them easily after all. They really don't know me at all, do they?

8.03 p.m.
Earlier today I texted Noah and Lily just to reassure them that I will definitely be there tomorrow to record the vlog. I expect that's put their minds at rest.

Sunday March 9th

10.20 a.m.
Mum and Dad have said I can invite Edgar here any time I wish. And somehow I managed to look extremely thrilled. I clearly have undiscovered acting talent.

11.01 a.m.
Only Elliot is suspicious.

'Why on earth are you going to Edgar's house?'

he demands.

'To get away from you, for a start.'

'But I won't be here,' says Elliot. 'I'm spending the day at my friend Marty's house.'

'And Marty has my deepest sympathy. But why shouldn't I visit a mate too?'

'Because you hate Edgar,' shouts Elliot.

'No I don't. In fact, I really enjoy hanging out with him.'

Elliot moves closer to me. 'Who are you?' he demands. 'And what have you done with the real Louis?'

I'm relieved to see Elliot leave for Marty's house shortly afterwards.

11.26 a.m.

When they make a film of my life (come on, it's got to happen, hasn't it?) I expect they will show the final countdown to when I escape from this house of horror in epic detail.

How am I feeling? Well, I'm excited and tense but most of all scared that at the very last moment something's going to happen to ruin everything.

12.02 p.m.

A woman who works with Mum (plus her hubby) has just turned up for a coffee, and I'm

105

immediately worried. What if this delays lunch? Well, it can't. I have to be out of here on the dot of two o'clock.

1.40 p.m.
The couple, Samantha and Greg, have stayed for a free meal. Yikes, I thought, but they got stuck in right away. And it's totally distracted my parents, who are charging about with extra food and drinks, with me helping them.

And then something dead strange happened.

Samantha started talking about Noah and Lily. That was a shock, I tell you. But apparently her daughter is a big fan of them. You should have seen the smiles freeze on my parents' faces when they heard that.

'And,' went on Samantha, 'I know you've been on their vlog twice, haven't you, Louis?'

'Three times actually,' I grinned. 'But who's counting?'

'So we're eating with a star then,' cooed Samantha.

I smiled modestly. 'I like to live simply.'

'I hear you were hilarious too,' said Samantha. 'In fact, my daughter and her friends were raving about you.'

A very odd look flashed across Mum's face. Was it guilt? I really think it might have been.

'And when will you be appearing with Noah and Lily again?' Samantha asked me.

For a mad moment I wanted to shout out, 'In about two hours' time.' But it was far, far too risky, so instead I let Mum answer for me.

'Louis will be returning when he can spare the time from all his other activities,' she said softly.

1.58 p.m.
I was just leaving the house when Mum called me back.

I paused, holding my breath. But Mum was smiling. 'Say hello to Edgar for us.'

'Of course I will.'

Then Mum spotted the school books under my arm (yeah, I'd remembered). 'And don't work too hard this afternoon.'

I could certainly reassure her on that point.

And that was it.

I was out!

1.59 p.m.
I expect for the film version they'll need to make it a bit more tense.

2.09 p.m.
I sped to Edgar's house. He was waiting on the

drive, beside the taxi.

'Hey, cheers for this,' I said, grinning away at him.

But no smile from Edgar. He just looked grumpy and fed-up. I shall definitely cut him from the film.

'And don't worry,' I said. 'I will pay you back. Could you lend me—'

'I'm coming with you,' he interrupted. And as he announced this he looked even more depressed, if that was possible.

Being cooped up with Edgar for twenty whole minutes would send me insane. So I said hastily, 'No need – and anyway I'm sure you'd much rather stay at home, rattling off more poems.'

Edgar raised his head haughtily. 'I have never *rattled off* poems, as you put it, and I haven't written one for several days. This afternoon I actually intended spending time repairing a model of Concorde for an elderly neighbour. But I promised Maddy I would accompany you.'

'Did you? She never said.' Thinking fast, I added, 'You'll be very bored.'

'I have no doubt of that, but Maddy insisted. Shall we depart?'

It might have been worse, I suppose. He could have brought some of his poems to recite aloud.

Still pretty awful, though.

What was Maddy thinking?

2.20 p.m.
I did try to converse with Edgar. 'You said you hadn't written any poems for several days. Why is that?'

'I'm blocked,' he snapped.

Trying to lighten the atmosphere, I declared, 'Our kitchen sink's always getting blocked. Maybe you need a plunger.' Then I laughed to myself.

'I didn't expect intelligent conversation,' said Edgar, 'and I haven't been disappointed.'

Snotty brainbox, I thought. But I had to admit, if he hadn't coughed up the extra money I'd be messing about with buses now.

So I said, 'Cheers again for the loan.'

'Maddy asked me.'

'Good old Maddy,' I said. 'I bet, like me, you still really miss her.'

'Of course I do,' he replied angrily. 'What a stupid ...' – his voice wavered – '... question.' Then he stared fiercely out of the window and I realised he was doing his very best not to cry.

I changed the subject. 'So what do you know about Noah and Lily?'

Edgar slowly turned away from the window. Then he took a deep breath. 'Not a thing. Never heard of them.'

'Wow.' I was genuinely amazed. 'I can't believe any teenager has never heard of Noah and Lily.'

'I march to a different beat to that of my contemporaries,' declared Edgar.

'O-kay,' I said slowly. 'Well, would you like me to tell you something about Noah and Lily?'

Edgar gave a very thin smile. 'You can never have too much knowledge, I suppose.'

2.31 p.m.
Edgar paid the taxi driver and asked him to return in forty-five minutes. We both got out.

I stood in front of Noah's house and felt a real sense of achievement.

Despite everything, I'd made it here.

I could hear the movie voice-over in my head.

Just one boy overcoming all the obstacles. Nothing can stop Louis. He is destined to succeed.

Chapter Fourteen
Grinning Gus

3.20 p.m.

After handing Edgar my school books, I rang the doorbell. I was in such a great mood, just like the first time I'd arrived here. It was Noah's mum who opened the door and exactly as before, she smiled so welcomingly and said, 'Welcome to our vlogging family.' The only difference was – well, this time she wasn't actually looking at me.

Instead her enthusiastic welcome was for someone else who'd just jumped out of a posh-looking car behind us – a boy a few years older than me, with a long thin face which looked even longer with his hair all gelled up.

And then I recognised him.

Grinning Gus.

He was an up-and-coming vlogger who always had funny things to say about his life. He didn't tell jokes exactly. It was more observations. He did challenges too, like when he ate a worm for breakfast. That went seriously viral!

But what was he doing here now?

I heard him say in his drawly way, 'Well, it'll be good to catch up with Noah and Lily again.'

'And they're so grateful to you,' said Noah's mum, 'for stepping in like this. Do come in.'

Grinning Gus slouched past Edgar and me. Then, baring his super gleaming gnashers at us, he scattered signed photographs, on which was scrawled 'I'm the dude, Grinning Gus' in our direction before strolling inside like an A-lister being ushered into a top nightclub.

'Please go through to the kitchen and make yourself at home, I shan't be a moment,' Noah's mum called after him.

By now a cold uneasiness was taking hold of me. Why was Noah's mum acting as if she couldn't see us? And why on earth had Grinning Gus popped up now? Surely we couldn't both be in the same vlog. Maybe they were recording two today?

Noah's mum turned back towards us. 'Louis,

what are you doing here?'

'I'm supposed to be here! I texted Noah and Lily to tell them I could make it. Didn't they tell you?'

'Your parents were very clear,' she replied. 'They said you are not to record any more vlogs until further notice.'

'But you can totally ignore that,' I said confidently. 'You see, my mum and dad had to attend two parents' evenings in two days. Well, of course this triggered off some very bizarre behaviour. They're fine again now though, and totally happy for me to appear today.'

Noah's mum pursed her lips disbelievingly. 'And if I call them now they'll back up your story.'

'Of course they will,' I said, 'but I don't want to put you to all that trouble. You're a busy lady, opening the door and all that. But if you don't believe me, ask him.' I pointed at Edgar. 'Have you ever seen a more honest face? Everything I say is true, isn't it, Edgar?'

A startled-looking Edgar swallowed hard. 'I can verify his story,' he said in a tight, low voice. After which he had a small coughing fit.

'There you are,' I said confidently.

Noah's mum took a long hard look at me before saying, 'I'm very sorry, Louis, but they've got someone else for today. But I'll make a bargain with you. If you both go home right away I shan't tell your parents you—'

'Will you at least let me see Noah and Lily ... just for a minute?' I interrupted desperately.

'But they're just about to record,' she insisted. 'I really must go.'

With that the door was closed firmly in our faces.

'Noah!' I yelled out suddenly.

'Why on earth are you shouting in the street?' demanded Edgar.

I thought that was obvious. 'I'm calling for Noah. He said I was his mischievous mate.' I yelled again, 'Noah!'

'Stop this racket at once.' Edgar's voice was nearly as loud as mine. 'Noah is not your mate.'

'How do you know? You've never even met him. You hadn't heard of him until half an hour ago.'

Edgar tutted. 'He has had plenty of opportunities to contact you and has manifestly failed to do so. Now I am calling the taxi so we can commence our return journey. And you can leave with your dignity intact at least.'

I wanted to argue with Edgar.

But for once I couldn't.

3.30 p.m.
Just zoned out in the taxi home, hardly saying
a word to Edgar. He sat bolt upright beside me,
looking nearly as miserable as I felt. The taxi
pulled up outside Edgar's house. He paid the
fare and we both slouched out.

Edgar solemnly handed me my school books
and then asked, 'What am I supposed to do with
this?' He held up Grinning Gus's signed poster
as if it were a particularly disgusting bogey.

'Stick it up on your wall,' I grinned.

Edgar actually gave a short laugh before
unexpectedly asking, 'Would you like to come
back into my house and look at my rocks?'

I thought I'd misheard him.

'There is a piece of agate I would especially
recommend,' he continued. 'You pick it up and
then just hold it in your hand while remembering
how it has been that shape for millions of years.
This immediately puts all your problems and
disappointments into perspective.'

And you know what, Edgar was completely
serious. Somehow I swallowed down a smile.
'Another time maybe,' I said.

3.50 p.m.
'Back already? Had a good afternoon?' asked
Mum cheerily.

115

'No, you totally wrecked it,' I wanted to reply. I would have done if I thought they'd feel bad. But I knew Mum and Dad would just freak out at me for going to Noah's house, plus I sort of liked that they knew nothing about my secret life today. (Noah's mum seems to have kept her word.)

But I won't forget what they've done to me. It's definitely going in the autobiography. That's if there ever will be one now – with my life going back to normal. *NORMAL*. The most horrible word ever, after 'homework' and 'school' and 'detention'. And 'Dunky', of course.

6.45 p.m.
Just done something very stupid. I watched Noah and Lily's latest vlog. Yeah, the one I should have been on. Don't ask me why. And, of course, it was horrible. Well, for me it was. Noah and Lily seemed to be having a fantastic time with their new best friend, Grinning Gus. Never once mentioned me. At the end they declared that Grinning Gus is their new regular agony uncle. So I'm well and truly dumped.

They also announced that they'd had such an awesome response to the awful beret Lily had designed for Noah – and which he was still wearing – that a limited number were now for sale for twenty-five pounds each. I wouldn't give you twenty-five bogeys for one!

And I'll never watch or read anything about Noah and Lily again. Too many memories.

9.20 p.m.

Just before my phone was taken away for the night a text arrived from Maddy. I'd given her the gory details of this afternoon of course. But she hardly mentioned it. Instead she wrote — well, look, here it is.

Louis, forget about today. Have discovered something far more exciting. This could totally make all your dreams come true. Need to talk to you tomorrow urgently. There's not much time. Love, Maddy.

What an incredible message.

And what is this really exciting thing that could make all my dreams come true?

Can't wait to find out.

Chapter Fifteen

Secret Audition

Monday March 10th
8.30 p.m.

Maddy has just Skyped me.

She read aloud, '"Are you under sixteen?"'

'So they tell me.'

'"And have you dreamed of breaking into show business, but have absolutely no acting experience?"'

'Correct again,' I whispered.

'"Well, this is your once in a lifetime chance, Louis." It doesn't actually say "Louis",' Maddy added unnecessarily.

She went on to explain how this American company, Castel Films, is making a movie in Britain. It's set in an American school near Winchester. So most of the actors would obviously be American. But there's a small but key role featuring a British boy. The actor scheduled to play this part had to pull out at the very last minute. So they'd decided to cast a total unknown.

'Now listen to this, Louis,' cried Maddy. 'The British character is very good-humoured and cheeky, and is often in trouble because he likes more than anything else to make people laugh ...' She stopped. 'Has the picture frozen?' she asked.

'No ... no, it's just ...' My voice began to shake. 'I can't believe it. It's me, isn't it?'

'Oh, Louis, it so is.' Then neither of us could speak for a moment. Finally Maddy read on, 'Just send us a five-minute show reel with you talking, performing, interacting with friends ... anything which shows us why you are right for this part. What we're looking for is someone with bags of personality which jumps off the screen.' Maddy stopped reading and looked right at me. 'So you haven't got to act all, Louis. Just be yourself.'

'I'll tell loads of jokes ...' I began.

Maddy nodded enthusiastically. 'The only thing is – and I've only just discovered this – the closing day is really soon. This Thursday – the thirteenth.'

'That's OK, there's still time,' I said. 'I'll film it tomorrow and whiz it straight off to you. I've been recording little bits of my act on my phone actually and—'

'Stuff from a phone can look very wobbly,' interrupted Maddy. 'I think you need it on a proper camera …'

'Which I haven't got.'

'No, but Edgar has,' said Maddy.

'And you think he'd lend it to me?'

'I'm sure he would, but I want you to borrow Edgar as well. I mean, get him to film it.'

A few days ago I wouldn't even have considered involving Edgar. But since yesterday I've had a few almost kindly thoughts about him. Perhaps he isn't quite as exceptionally annoying as I thought he was.

Maddy went on, 'Edgar is very skilled with his camera and he can zoom in and out at just the right moment.'

'Just so long as he doesn't recite a poem while he's doing it,' I said. Then I added, 'You do know, Maddy, that you have total world rights to my career for ever, don't you?'

*   *   *

8.50 p.m.
There's just one problem – my parents. I daren't tell them what I'm doing. They're so into their super-parenting right now they'd say a big fat NO to me auditioning. So instead I'm going to pretend Edgar is just coming round tomorrow to hang out with me.

8.51 p.m.
So I must warn Edgar to hide his camera as well.

9.08 p.m.
Just received a text from Edgar. He says he realises the importance of being undercover and he will spare no effort in assisting me tomorrow to get round my parents' ban. Even he realises this is definitely it.

9.09 p.m.
Who needs Noah and Lily – when Fate is calling me to be a movie star?

Tuesday March 11th

4.40 p.m.
Mum and Dad are delighted Edgar is dropping in tonight. They think he will be a good influence on me. Only Elliot is once again suspicious.

'What's going on? Why have you invited him round?' he demanded.

'I must be turning into an intellectual,' I replied.

4.55 p.m.
I told my parents Edgar is very shy, so I'd appreciate not having people stomping in and out of my bedroom when he's here.

'You're really quite sensitive to other people, aren't you?' said Dad.

6.50 p.m.
Edgar has arrived, carrying a large bag of rocks. 'I've brought all the ones you wanted to see, including a particularly fine fire opal.'

'Oh brilliant, can't wait to examine your fire opal,' I replied, enjoying my parents' look of total amazement.

Upstairs Edgar hissed excitedly, 'As I suspected, my rock collection totally camouflaged this.' And from the bottom of his bag he brought out an extremely impressive camera.

7.25 p.m.
Edgar started filming right away.

'Hey, I'm not ready yet.'

'It's all right, I'm not filming you,' said Edgar

as his camera zoomed all around my bedroom.

'What are you doing then?' I asked.

'Creating atmosphere. Very important,' he said.

7.48 p.m.

At last I began my act. Smiling into the camera, I said, 'How are you doing? I'm Louis, also known as Louis the Laugh. And I love crazy, stupid jokes such as:

'Why should you take a pencil to bed? *To draw the curtains.*'

'Excuse me,' interrupted Edgar. 'Little tip for you.'

'Go on,' I growled.

'Try and not move your arms about so much. It's very distracting.'

'Thanks so much,' I muttered.

'Just trying to be helpful,' replied Edgar.

I continued. 'Why did the boy throw the clock out of the window? *He wanted to see time fly.*'

'Excuse me again,' said Edgar, 'but you lowered your voice at the end and so lost your punchline. Would you mind doing it again?'

'For you, Edgar, anything,' I said through gritted teeth.

I repeated the joke and managed one more – *Doctor, doctor, I keep thinking I'm a dog. How long has this been going on? Ever since I was a puppy!'* – before Edgar said, 'Sorry to interrupt again but I've got an important question for you. Can you tell any funnier jokes?'

'These are funny!' I cried indignantly.

Edgar shook his head. 'Do you know what I think?'

'I know you're going to tell me.'

'I think you should just talk naturally into the camera about dreams and ambitions.' The camera zoomed in on me hopefully.

'Too boring,' I scowled.

'Not at all, this will give them an insight into who you really are.'

'They will get that by watching me perform.'

'But what are you performing? Stale, tired jokes,' said Edgar pityingly.

'Do you know when I like you best, Edgar?' My voice rose. 'When you are not here.'

We glared at each other. Then suddenly I spotted Dad hovering in my bedroom doorway. Instantly I grabbed one of the rocks, which glinted in my hands. I glanced at it for a moment and then asked, 'So how many million years old could this be, Edgar? Oh, hi, Dad,' I added, as if I'd just spotted him. 'I'm helping Edgar make a film about his rock collection,' I explained.

'They've been arguing very loudly,' proclaimed

Elliot, who had bounced in as well.

'No, we've been debating.' I turned to Dad. 'I had no idea rocks could be so interesting.'

Dad beamed. 'You see, Louis, what happens when you open yourself up to new interests.'

'Yes, I see that now, Dad,' I said.

'Now who would like some refreshments?'

'I'd much rather we continued filming, please,' said Edgar.

'Of course, carry on then, lads.' Dad left, but Elliot lingered, staring at us very curiously for a moment, before going too.

'If you'd ever really like me to talk to you about rocks—' began Edgar.

'Not a chance,' I interrupted. 'Now will you just film my act?'

'If those are your wishes,' he sighed.

'They really are,' I said.

8.09 p.m.

Finally I was able to rattle through five of my very best jokes. Not a glimmer of a smile from Edgar, of course.

'If you want to laugh at all,' I said to him, 'feel free.'

'Perhaps,' said Edgar, 'you would be kind enough to make some sort of gesture when you have reached the punchline.'

'How about if I dangle one of my eyeballs?'

Somehow I finished my act. I think it was quite funny, but was it hilarious enough to win the glorious prize? Then I wondered if I should do it again, but Edgar was already packing up.

'Can you edit together all the funny parts of my performance?' I asked.

'Leave it to me,' said Edgar.

The trouble is, he doesn't know anything about comedy.

Wednesday March 12th

7.00 p.m.
Poppy rings.

She'll want to know what I thought of her on that BBC variety show.

And the awful truth is that I forgot to watch it. Well, so much has happened lately. But that's no excuse. And if I admit that now she'll think I'm a rubbish friend.

So I say dead fast, 'Hey, Poppy, I've got to say you were sensational on Sunday.'

'Really?' She sounds stunned. But then she is very modest.

So I really pile it on now. 'You've been great before, but on that show you were the best you've ever been. In fact, I've forgotten all the

126

other acts. You completely stole it.'

'Well, that's very interesting,' Poppy says slowly, 'because I didn't actually appear on the TV on Sunday.'

'Are you sure?' I squeak.

'Positive.'

'But then I've got a different telly to yours so I probably picked up the uncut version ...'

'Louis, I wasn't cut. But I can't tell you what happened over the phone.'

'Why, is your line being bugged or something?'

'Can I come round and see you tomorrow?'

'Of course you can, though I'm amazed you want to after me lying my head off to you.'

She laughs. 'I thought it was kind of cute.'

Then I ask, 'But you are all right, Poppy?'

'I'll explain everything tomorrow.'

Then she firmly changes the subject to Noah and Lily's latest vlog and why on earth wasn't I on it.

8.50 p.m.

Edgar has sent the film to Maddy. 'And was it any good?' I asked her cautiously.

'It was brilliant.'

'Really! I didn't think I was that funny.'

'Oh, you were,' said Maddy. 'And Edgar captured every glorious second.' She sighed.

127

'It's going to feel like *ages* now till next week, when they decide who to see in person.' Then she started to giggle.

'What?' I demanded.

'Just remembering your performance. I have such high hopes for this, Louis. In fact, my agent antennae tell me this could be the winner.'

I was astonished. 'You really think that?'

'I totally do.'

'I must have been much funnier than I thought then.'

How very strange.

Chapter Sixteen

Awesome Land

Thursday March 13th

8.22 a.m.
Breakfast. I go into the kitchen and Mum and Dad immediately stop talking. This can only mean one thing.

'It's OK,' I say cheerily. 'You can carry on talking about me.'

Dad looks at Mum. Then she looks at Dad and says, 'We were just working out the best time to go into your school next week to talk to your teachers.'

Now that sentence is breathtakingly depressing anyway. But to be talking about school and my teachers before you've even finished your breakfast – well, I'm sure there's a law against that.

'Let me get this right,' I say. 'You only went to my parents' evening a few weeks ago and already you're putting in for another go.'

'We just want to see how you are progressing,' says Mum.

I shake my head at them. 'I can tell you now, Mum, all my teachers will think you're creepy and uncool bothering them so soon. You will not have a good time.'

But, of course, Mum and Dad don't listen to me.

If only I could break the spell they're trapped under. For their sakes as well as mine.

8.50 a.m.
You remember Jack, the new boy I've been helping. Well, we've hit it off and as he doesn't live far from me, I called for him this morning. His mum opened the door – she was very friendly – and said to come through as Jack was still eating his breakfast. You won't believe what he was eating. Only a great slab of chocolate accompanied by a massive helping of ice cream.

'You're allowed to eat that for breakfast?' I exclaimed.

'Of course.' Jack grinned at me. 'I can have it whenever I want.'

Also at the table was his little sister. She was finishing off a massive bowl of custard. She sighed happily as she slurped it down. Then she shouted, 'Want more custard!'

Her mum sped in. 'Aren't you worried, Maisie, that you might be sick again?'

'No I'm not,' she said firmly.

'All right, well, it's your choice, dear.'

Maisie and her mum headed for the fridge while I asked Jack, 'What's going on here?'

'Mum doesn't want to impose her views on us, that's all.'

'So you could have ice cream and chocolate for breakfast every single day?'

Jack nodded. 'Mum thinks in the end I'll get bored of this and move on to something much healthier. But she wants us to make that decision, not her,' he said. 'And whenever she can, Mum avoids saying no to me. She thinks it's bad for my "development".'

'And she's so right,' I sighed. 'I feel as if somehow I've wandered into Awesome Land. You are incredibly lucky, living here.' Then I thought of something else. 'So what about going to school?'

'Mum and I discussed this,' said Jack. 'And we

agreed that I do need to learn stuff. But Mum will never say, "Off to school now." I leave when I choose. She says she'd rather I understood for myself why I have to be on time.'

'And if one day you decided to have an extra holiday … ?'

'Mum wouldn't say a word.'

As we left, Maisie was on her third helping of custard.

1.20 p.m.

At school I had more questions for Jack.

'So was your mum always this brilliant?'

'Oh no. Until recently, she was just a normal moany parent,' Jack explained. 'But then she saw something on the internet about Yes Parenting.'

'Yes Parenting,' I muttered. 'I like it already.'

'So she went on a course about it and afterwards she said to me, "I see now why things have gone wrong between us. I haven't been saying yes to you enough".'

'I could never imagine my parents saying that to me,' I sighed.

'She thinks it's important for me to just discover who I am.'

'Can we swap parents?'

'Not a chance,' grinned Jack.

'Don't blame you,' I said. 'Especially as mine are completely caught up in "No Parenting" right now.'

4.00 p.m.
Walking home, Jack offered to find the details of that *Yes Parenting* course.

'But how would I get my mum and dad to go?' I asked.

'Tell them it's fun.'

'That would put them right off!' I said. 'Do you get a certificate for turning up?'

'I could find out,' said Jack.

'That might help.'

But as I reached Jack's house a much better plan jumped into my head.

Chapter Seventeen

Improving My Parents' Social Life

4.32 p.m.

The first part of my scheme went like a dream.

I told Jack's mum my parents would like to pop round tomorrow night and welcome her to the area.

'That's so kind of them,' gushed Jack's mum.

'They're very big-hearted,' I agreed. 'Take after me.'

'Shall I text them?' she asked.

I considered for a second. 'Best to let them just drop by,' I added. 'They don't like a fuss and if you could tell them how you like to say yes to your children at all times, I know they would be incredibly fascinated.'

5.12 p.m.
I thought the second part would be trickier. And it was.

'But we can't just barge in there tomorrow night uninvited!' exclaimed Mum.

'I keep telling you, you *have* been invited,' I said.

'And it's been such a busy week,' said Dad, 'we hadn't planned on going out—'

'The thing is,' I interrupted, 'Jack says since they moved here no one has come to visit his mum yet. Not a single person has called. Isn't that shocking?'

Mum did look a bit concerned, so I pressed on. 'Every day Jack sees his poor old mum waiting by the window, hoping today will be the day someone calls. But,' I lowered my voice to barely a whisper, 'no one ever does. So Jack's incredibly worried about her, especially as she's not getting any younger.'

'How old is she?' asked Mum.

'About thirty-five,' I said.

Mum and Dad both burst out laughing then, which wasn't the reaction I wanted at all, but Mum added, 'I'm sure you're exaggerating, but if Jack's mother has invited us all ...'

'She really has, and you won't regret this,' I interrupted eagerly. 'In fact, I wouldn't be surprised if tomorrow you don't both make a friend for life and she'll want to see you all the time.'

My parents didn't look as thrilled by this prediction as I'd expected. Still, they are going. And I'm sure half an hour in that atmosphere will be enough, and my highly impressionable parents will change back to those happy carefree times when they never bothered me at all.

6.35 p.m.
Wanted to speed through my homework tonight before Poppy came round. But Mum has to keep interfering. She read my essay on *Julius Caesar* by William Shakespeare, then announced she thought I could probe much deeper into the text. She even wrote out some suggestions. 'You can ignore them if you like.' But there was a real 'don't you dare' gleam in her eye as she said this.

The trouble is, my brain hurts already. Any more homework and it could well explode. And then I won't be able to help Poppy and it'll all be Mum's fault.

*   *   *

7.50 p.m.

Poppy arrived earlier with her grandad. But he announced that he wasn't stopping. 'I'll be back in a little while, but I want to give you two a chance to talk together.' Then he leaned forward and whispered in my ear, 'I know you will do your best for her.'

And Poppy's first words to me in the living room – which my parents had vacated for us – were, 'Poor Grandad, I can't make him understand why I couldn't appear on television last Sunday. In fact, no one understands. You're my last hope.'

'If I'm your last hope, then you really are in trouble,' I grinned. 'But spare me nothing. Tell me everything.'

'I was in my dressing room, all set to appear on television ...'

'A dream come true,' I chipped in.

'You don't need to remind me about that, Louis,' said Poppy sadly. 'I do realise what a chance I've thrown away.'

'So why did you then?'

'At the last minute I just couldn't move.'

'Nerves,' I said promptly.

To be dead honest, being sympathetic to Poppy was proving harder than I'd imagined. All my dreams had come crashing round my ears last Sunday. But Poppy – well, no one was stopping her but herself.

'And everyone gets nerves,' I said. 'Even I do. So next time, just—'

'You needn't go on about it,' interrupted Poppy sharply.

'I didn't think I was,' I muttered.

There was a distinctly awkward silence for a moment before Poppy cried, 'The worst thing is, I know I've let Grandad down.' She began to shake then, as tears spilled down her face.

I leapt up and crouched down by her chair. 'Hey, come on,' I began.

'No, it's all right, Louis. I know my life as a magician is over.'

'What are you talking about?' Then I added, 'There's something you're not telling me, isn't there?'

She nodded slowly.

'Well, come on, I'm all ears. I mean, I really am.'

She gave a small smile. 'You know how people leave you messages on your website and most of them are really lovely. But a couple of people have put up stuff recently about how I'm only on television because I'm in a wheelchair and people feel sorry for me—'

'What total rubbish,' I interrupted.

'They also think I'm a very overrated magician.'

'Poppy, they're only jealous ... I hope you deleted them right away,' I added.

'Of course. I didn't want Grandad seeing what they said, as it would only have upset him. And I really thought I'd forgotten about them, Louis. But just before I was due to go on, everything they'd said came rushing back into my head. Only this time I found myself agreeing with them.'

'Oh, Poppy.'

'Then my mind went completely blank. I couldn't even remember the order of my magic tricks. I knew I'd be really clumsy and my timing would be completely off. There was no way I could go out there.'

'And so you didn't,' I said sadly.

'But the producer was really understanding. She's even given me another chance this Sunday.'

'That's good. Fantastic, in fact, isn't it?'

'But what if it happens again and I start remembering all the nasty comments? What do I do then, Louis?'

I stood up and started pacing about, thinking for a few moments. 'What you need is another voice to drown them out. Mine.'

Poppy looked at me eagerly. 'So you'll go with me on Sunday?'

'Of course I will,' I replied. 'And you can rely on me to keep saying the opposite of those trolls. Dead loudly too.'

She laughed suddenly.

'What is it?' I asked.

'You've cheered me up already.' Then her face darkened. 'It won't be easy though.'

Chapter Eighteen
Yes Parenting

Friday March 14th

4.55 p.m.
Elliot has had a meltdown.

It was brilliant.

Even on Friday the four of us have to play our recorders. 'We're not giving up. A breakthrough will come,' declared Dad. And it did – though not in the way he'd expected.

We were screeching our tuneless way through 'Three Blind Mice' (yeah, we're still on that one, lucky us) when Elliot suddenly flung his recorder on the ground. 'No! No! No!' he yelled. 'I can't take it any more! I hate playing the recorder!

It's ruining my life!' And he stormed off.

Dad shook his head very sadly. 'We only wanted you and Elliot to see that with a bit of effort—'

'We could sound worse than ever,' I interrupted.

5.20 p.m.
Mum and Dad chatted with Elliot in his bedroom for ages. Then Dad came downstairs and announced to me, 'Your mum and I are good listeners.' I raised my eyebrows as high as they would go. 'And we have decided to suspend our recorder sessions for now.'

Could the super-parenting spell be starting to fade at last?

Well, just wait until they've had an evening of Yes Parenting.

8.15 p.m.
In the car, after telling Elliot to stop fiddling with his hair, which she had wetted down to stop it sticking up all over the place, Mum asked me again, 'Are you sure Jack's mum is expecting us?'

'Jack says she's talked of nothing else,' I replied. 'She can't believe someone is visiting her at last.'

But as the car pulled up, Jack leapt forward and nodded at me to talk to him privately. He whispered, 'Much better if you came back tomorrow?'

'Why?' I demanded not unreasonably.

'Trust me, you don't want to take your parents in there now. Maisie is having the tantrum to end all tantrums. And it's not pretty.'

Thinking fast, I announced to my family, 'Would you believe it, Jack's mum and sister have just gone down with a highly contagious stomach bug.'

'It's terrible in there,' added Jack helpfully. 'The house stinks and there's puke and all sorts everywhere—'

'OK. Thanks, Jack. We get the picture,' I interrupted.

'And is it just you looking after them both?' asked Mum.

Jack nodded and for some reason he seemed unable to talk any more. Instead he quickly turned away from us.

'Is there anything we can do?' asked Dad, looking in some concern at Jack, who was now shaking and could just manage a wordless squeak in reply. Only I realised he'd got the giggles.

So I said very quickly, 'We'll call round again

143

soon, mate, when your mum's better.'

That's when Jack's mum appeared.

'You should be tucked up in bed,' called my mum, 'with a hot drink.'

Looking more than a bit startled, Jack's mum stuttered, 'Should I ... why?'

'Well, you've got—' began Mum, and then gawped at the figure glowing with health in front of her. 'You haven't got flu, have you?'

'Whoever told you that?' asked Jack's mum.

'Your son,' said Dad, 'for some reason.'

There was a second of silence which lasted several hours and then Jack burst into fits of laughter.

'Youthful high spirits, I'm sure,' smiled Jack's mum.

'Mmm,' murmured my parents doubtfully.

Jack's mum went on, 'It's so good of you to come round and welcome me to the area. Do come in.'

'Well, we wanted you to know we really are friendly here,' said Mum.

'Oh, I know that already,' cried Jack's mum, 'because everyone has been so lovely. Only tonight, Eileen, the lady two doors down, came round with a cake she'd baked for us. Wasn't that a kind gesture?'

'It certainly was,' replied Mum giving me a

HORRIBLE glare.

Inside the house we were greeted by a very loud wailing sound, like a human burglar alarm. In fact, it was Jack's sister, Maisie.

'Oh, Maisie, please stop this now,' cried Jack's mum, rushing into the kitchen where Maisie was sitting at the table with her arms folded in front of a plate of food and shrieking away.

'Yeah, shut up!' yelled Jack.

Maisie paused in her yelling to stick her tongue out at him.

Jack's mum explained to my parents. 'Maisie's a vegetable refuser. Well, they both are at the moment. I let Jack off tonight but I suggested to Maisie she try some of them, as vegetables are so good for her. Really I just wanted to open up a conversation with her about her diet and—'

'She's been in a foul mood since she came home from school,' interrupted Jack.

'No I haven't!' shouted Maisie. 'And I hate you!'

Jack's mum raised a hand. 'It was my fault, Maisie dear. You needn't eat anything you don't want.'

Maisie promptly pushed her plate away gleefully.

'How lucky are you!' cried Elliot in some wonderment. 'I hate vegetables and I'm made to

145

eat them every day.'

Maisie smirked and then got down from her chair. 'Don't you want to finish any of your meal?' asked her mum.

'Maybe. But not right now.'

I could feel Mum and Dad beside me, struggling to contain their amazement. They'd never let Elliot – or me – be picky over our food like that.

'Now, who would like a drink?' asked Jack's mum.

'Not for us, we only came round for a minute,' Mum glared at me again, 'to say hello and—'

'I want a glass of lemonade,' interrupted Elliot. 'A big glass.'

'Please,' cut in Dad.

Elliot didn't say a word.

'It's all right,' said Jack's mum. 'He'll say please when he's ready.'

'He's ready now,' said Mum sternly.

Jack's mum handed Elliot a large glass of lemonade, which he gulped down noisily.

'Elliot, please don't drink like that,' said Mum.

Elliot ignored that, smacked his lips appreciatively and declared, 'It's so great here.'

'It really is,' I agreed. 'Such a super, happy atmosphere,' I went on, although there wasn't much sign of that at the moment. I turned to

Jack's mum. 'How come you have such a happy family? What's your secret?'

'There's no secret,' she smiled. 'It's just I want to say a big yes to who my children actually are.'

'How very interesting.' I gave my parents a highly significant look. 'Wanting-to-say-yes-to-who-your-children-actually-are.' I repeated this very slowly so that my parents could really take it in. 'Tell us more.'

'I let my children be children,' Jack's mum went on, 'and find their own way. My main job is to be fully present with them ...'

She was interrupted by Maisie rushing in. 'Come and see what I've just done in the living room,' she demanded.

Jack's mum smiled indulgently. 'She's taking such an interest in our new house. All right, we'll have a look.'

But her smile fell away when she saw what Maisie had actually done in the living room, while Jack let out a cry of total horror.

One whole wall was now covered in crayon drawings of what were supposed to be Jack, Maisie and their mum. There were also pictures of some flowers of retina-scorching brightness and an extremely odd-looking animal, which could have been a cow or a dog or possibly both. Mum and Dad stared at the wall. And kept on staring.

'Make her wash it off right now,' declared Jack, 'or I'll do it myself.'

'You won't.' Maisie bristled with the pride of a true artist. 'And I'm going to decorate all the walls like that because it's lovely, isn't it?' She confidently asked this question of everyone except Jack.

Mum and Dad just swallowed nervously, while Elliot chuckled away as if he were watching a favourite comedy show.

'It's wonderful you have this urge to create,' began Jack's mum.

'I'm not sitting in here with that garbage on the walls,' interrupted Jack.

'And I'm thrilled you are exploring your talent,' Maisie's mum went on, 'but Jack clearly has strong opinions about this also, and that's good too. So what I would suggest is that later we open up a conversation about this.'

But Jack had already opened up his conversation by snatching the box of crayons out of Maisie's grip.

'They're mine, give them back!' she screamed.

'That is not the way we communicate,' cried Jack's mum, then added desperately, 'I think it's definitely time for a group hug.'

Instead Jack waved the crayons in Maisie's

face. 'Sorry, everyone, but my sister just isn't up to Yes Parenting. I'd really recommend it though.' Then he tore upstairs, closely followed by a yelling Maisie.

Elliot made as if to join in the fun until Mum said, 'We must go, I'm afraid ... it's been lovely meeting you all.'

'It really has,' agreed Dad with all the insincerity of an adult.

'You must come again,' offered Jack's mum. 'I'm afraid things can get a little crazy here occasionally.'

The yells and screams grew louder. 'I think you'd better go and be fully present upstairs,' said Mum.

We saw ourselves out.

Saturday March 15th

Just witnessed a revolting sight. My parents being extremely pleased with themselves.

They rolled around the house saying stuff like, 'It's very useful to say no to children, otherwise they have no idea how to react when they're told no in the real world.'

And ...

Actually, I'll spare you any more. Just because I have to listen to it all day long doesn't mean you have to as well.

I worked so hard getting them to Jack's house yesterday. And you know what, it's only made them worse than ever.

Chapter Nineteen
Poppy's Bombshell

Sunday March 16th

1.50 p.m.
Arrived at the studios with Poppy and her grandad about twenty minutes ago. Already they've been whisked away to rehearse. So I'm just hanging about in the waiting room. But it's still exciting to be at a TV studio. Not as exciting as being in a Noah and Lily vlog, of course. But I'm not thinking about that. So let's not mention it again.

2.12 p.m.
Poppy's grandad dropped by to tell me Poppy

is in make-up now. He looks as dapper as ever, with a red rose curling out of the buttonhole of his grey suit. He handed me some sandwiches and a drink. He said it's important to keep me fed and watered, as I'm a vital person here today. When I said I haven't done anything, he replied that knowing I was here, supporting her, meant the world to Poppy.

2.25 p.m.
Just visited Poppy in her very own dressing room. She looked great, with her long hair all brushed down on one side ('her mermaid look', I call it). She was dead happy too, because the rehearsal had 'gone like a breeze'. Grandad said he was certain the live show would be even better. It starts at 3 p.m. Poppy is on at 3.15 p.m. Grandad and I will be in the audience, cheering like crazy.

2.40 p.m.
Can't believe this.
   Poppy is refusing to go on AGAIN. Her grandad has just been talking to her. Suddenly he looks ten years older, poor guy. 'If Poppy pulls out again today people will start saying she is unreliable and it will really damage her career,' he said.

So now he's asked me to speak to her.

3.04 p.m.
Poppy was in a dark corner of the dressing room, slumped forward in her chair. She was a completely different person from the confident, assured one I'd seen barely thirty minutes before. Just seeing her like that gave me a knot in my stomach. She managed an awful little laugh when she saw me. 'I warned you, Louis, that this would happen. But I was doing so well until ...'

'You've had another one of those nasty messages, haven't you?'

It was a wild guess. But Poppy immediately looked up.

'I was just messing about on my phone and there it was:

Always remember you're nowhere near as good as people think you are. You're just a fluke and only there because people pity you.

And I know you'll say, Louis, that they're jealous and, they probably are, but that doesn't mean they can't be right as well, does it? Anyway, my mind's gone totally blank again.' She gave another awful laugh. 'Right now I'm not even sure what my own name is.' She rushed on in this low, flat voice. 'I'll just humiliate myself –

153

and Grandad – if I go on now. So will you ask him to take me home?'

Poppy was allowing some troll to totally crush her. But I couldn't let that happen to her. Somehow I had to spark her back to life.

'Will you find Grandad,' she persisted, 'and explain it to him?'

'Yes,' I said very quietly. 'I think I can make him understand why you can't go on.'

'I'm very grateful.'

'Well, will you do me a favour then?' I asked, walking over to her.

'Of course I will.'

'Let me go on in your place?'

Poppy hadn't been expecting that at all. She sat very still for a moment. 'But you're not prepared,' she said at last.

'Doesn't matter. I've got a million jokes in my head. The difficulty will be getting me off the stage. So will you do it?'

'Well, I'll try,' she began. 'I mean Julie, the producer, may not be very keen. Last time they just replaced me with—'

'Try your hardest to persuade her,' I said, 'because this is the very, very greatest thing that's ever happened to you. And as you don't want it ...'

'I never said I didn't want it,' corrected Poppy.

'I said I know I won't be any good.'

'And I know I'll be superb. Thank you so much for this, Poppy. This really is an opportunity in a million.' I swaggered to the door.

Suddenly Poppy whirled round in her wheelchair and sped towards me. 'Louis, stop! You're not going out there.'

I spun round. 'Try and stop me.'

We were still glaring at each other when her grandad appeared in the doorway. 'It's time for you to get ready to go on, my dear. I will, of course, do whatever you want, as I have never pushed you. At least, I sincerely hope I haven't. But this is—'

'An opportunity in a million,' interrupted Poppy. 'And that's why I'm ready.'

'Are you really?' I asked, in a voice dripping with disappointment.

Poppy looked up at me and grinned. 'You're overacting now, Louis. But you had me going there for a few moments. In fact, you got me so mad ...'

'Meant every word,' I replied, grinning. 'Now go out there and make me and that troll insanely jealous.'

5.06 p.m.
She did that all right.

The audience didn't just applaud her at the end. No, they gave her a standing ovation. And she was colossally brilliant, especially that last trick where she tore a newspaper into tiny pieces and then, totally incredibly, seemingly out of thin air she held up the very same newspaper completely intact. How did she do that? The audience just went wild. No wonder her grandad was weeping into his giant handkerchief.

There was so much fuss afterwards that Poppy and her grandad had to stay on for more interviews. So I had a taxi home, all to myself.

And I sat in the back remembering Poppy's face at the end, with all that applause raining down on her. What a moment!

Chapter Twenty

Super Swot

Monday March 17th

5.20 p.m.
Mum and Dad were late home.

'I know where you've been,' I called out. One glance at their dejected faces told me everything. I shook my head at them. 'Why did you do it?'

'We just wanted an update on your progress,' said Mum.

'I suppose you saw Dunky,' I asked.

'We did have a brief word with Mr Duncan.'

'Let me guess exactly what he said: "Louis hasn't made any progress and never will. Now go away for ever."'

'No,' said Dad. 'He's detected a very small improvement in your work. All the teachers have.'

But the air hummed with their disappointment. I know what Mum and Dad had hoped to hear. That I'd transformed into Super Swot and was now, in fact, the brainbox of the entire school.

The only way I'll ever be top of a class is if I'm put into a class of two-year-olds.

But I've got other talents. Well, one – I can entertain people. Why isn't that enough for my parents?

9.00 p.m.
Three days to go until Castel Films announce who they have chosen to audition for the top film role. Maddy and I have just been talking about it.

'They'll probably send you an email or they might leave a voicemail message,' she said. She was being incredibly confident. 'So be ready, won't you?'

'I was born ready,' I replied. 'It's just … I'm not sure my jokes were that funny.'

'Why won't you believe me?' said Maddy. 'You were hilarious.'

Tuesday March 18th

A present has arrived from Poppy. The biggest joke book I've ever seen. (Quick sample: *How can you kill someone with an egg? Eggsterminate them.*)

Inside she wrote: 'To Louis, a truly loyal friend. Love, Poppy. P.S. Your turn next. It must be.'

Only two days until Castel Films say who they've picked.

Wednesday March 19th

5.30 p.m.

The revolution has started.

Dad announced we have a music tutor coming round tomorrow at seven o'clock to teach us the recorder.

'No, no, no!' yelled Elliot, leaping up. And for once I was in complete solidarity with him. The thought of hearing 'Three Blind Mice' again made me feel ill.

'Haven't we abandoned the recorder owing to the noise-polluting racket we all make?' I asked.

'Does this family ever give up?' replied Dad jauntily.

The response was a resounding silence from

everyone, even Mum at first. At last she said faintly, 'Of course we don't.'

'So I've rethought how we can achieve our goal, and it's with a music teacher.' Dad smiled triumphantly.

But to my huge surprise, Mum said, 'I'm not sure tomorrow is a good idea as I might be working late. I did tell you.'

'And it's not a good idea for Elliot and me either,' I said firmly, 'especially as our eardrums still haven't recovered from the last battering.'

'All right, fine, I'll see this tutor – who is supposed to be excellent, by the way – on my own and get some tips for us all,' said Dad.

'So we don't have to see him?' I was keen to get this absolutely clear.

'Well, you can say hello to him.'

'I'd much rather say goodbye to him,' I said. 'And Dad, try to keep the noise down, will you?'

6.50 p.m.
By this time tomorrow I'll know if I have been picked for the big audition. In fact, Maddy thinks they'll probably contact me in the morning, but the afternoon is a possibility too.

An email is most likely.

Can you imagine the agony of having to wait for that ping all day long?

Keep everything crossed for me.

Thursday March 20th

9.05 a.m.
Jack is so gutted. Yes Parenting is over in his house.

He told me it ended yesterday afternoon. This is what happened. Jack's mum had said he and Maisie could design their bedrooms exactly how they wanted. 'This will help you gain in confidence as well as teach you how to make decisions,' she said.

But when his mum saw Jack's bedroom walls covered in dripping black paint and Maisie's decorated with odd-looking creatures which she claimed were aliens, she shrieked, 'I'm sorry but I'm saying no to your bedroom walls.'

'You've said "no" to us,' cried Jack.

His mum went on to say that they could suggest ideas for their rooms but she alone would decide if they fitted in with the decor of the house.

'But what about us gaining in confidence and making decisions for ourselves?' demanded Jack.

'It's time you learn another life skill,' she replied. 'How to compromise.' Tragically, Jack's mum looked really happy as she said this.

6.42 p.m.
Not going to drag this out.
  I'll tell you right away.
  Zilch.
  Zero.
  Nothing from Castel Films.
  Don't want to write much more except to say
I will not give up. So don't be too downhearted.
To cheer you up a joke (from Poppy's present):

What type of boats do vampires use?
  Blood vessels.

  I wish I'd told that one on my audition tape.

6.46 p.m.
Did I say I will not give up?

7.35 p.m.
Mum was late home so we had just finished
eating when the doorbell rang. Dad's music
teacher, I thought. Well, I'm staying well away
from him, so I shot upstairs. Rain streamed
drearily down the windows, so even the weather
matched my mood.
  And I was pretty annoyed when I was called

downstairs. In fact, I nearly didn't go. Mum and Dad were in the hallway chatting to the music teacher. He had a big suntanned face and was wearing a very expensive-looking suit with a massive brightly coloured scarf round his neck. He looked like a cross between an Italian football manager and Doctor Who. And when he saw me he cracked a huge smile.

'Here he is, here's Louis.' He seemed absolutely delighted by my presence. Well, it didn't matter. My lips weren't going near a recorder tonight. 'It's such a pleasure to meet you,' he went on, 'as I bring you fantastically good news.'

Chapter Twenty-One
Mystery Caller

He continued, 'I'm Jimmy James. Sounds as if I have two first names, doesn't it? But I'll tell you, no one ever forgets it.'

Then he laughed heartily while we all gawped at him in total bewilderment. And I realised this probably wasn't the music teacher. But who was he and why exactly was he here?

He then waved this dead flashy card about and announced, 'I'm the casting director from Castel Films.'

At that point I nearly choked with excitement. He'd turned up at my house to tell me I'd won the chance to audition. Surely that was the most likely explanation, and yet I hardly dared believe it.

Somehow I managed to say, 'Well, Jimmy James, may I introduce my housemates, technically known as my mum and dad. I can thoroughly recommend them. And that little prune coming out of the kitchen is my brother, Elliot. I can't recommend him at all.'

Jimmy James threw back his head and laughed and then boomed, 'Now may I impose on your hospitality and ask if we can sit down somewhere? I have so much to tell you. And I think you're going to like it.'

In a total trance Mum and Dad led him into the living room. Jimmy James spread out on the sofa, taking off his scarf and placing it beside him. He leaned back, instantly at home. 'Well, folks, I hope you don't think it's a big imposition me turning up unannounced like this. But I get such a kick out of moments like this.' He beamed around.

'I'm afraid,' said Mum, her voice rising, 'we are totally and completely in the dark. What has Castel Films got to do with Louis?'

'Let me explain to you good folks,' said Jimmy James. 'Now, you know your son auditioned to be in an American movie, which is being filmed here in the UK.'

'No,' chorused Mum and Dad together.

Jimmy James chuckled as if they'd just said something incredibly hilarious. 'You don't remember Louis and his buddy sending off a five-minute audition tape to us?'

'They don't remember,' I explained, 'because they didn't know. I never told them.'

'That only makes this all the more interesting,' said Jimmy James, totally unfazed. 'I'm so delighted to tell you, Louis, that of all the audition tapes – and I assure you we've watched plenty – yours was *the one*. Well, we struck gold there. That's why we'd like you to audition for the role.'

You know how corks fly out of bottles. Well, right then my head felt as if it was taking off all by itself. I was so giddy with shock and joy I just took a deep intake of breath and gave a kind of whistle. Mum and Dad's mouths hung open too.

It was Elliot who piped up, 'Actually I'm much better at acting than him. I've been in four school plays and he hasn't been in any.'

Jimmy James grinned broadly. 'Loving that confidence.' Then he looked questioningly at me.

'Go on, speak,' I told myself. But it's hard when your head's in orbit. So I gurgled, 'Thank you very much,' sounding even younger than Elliot.

'We owe *you* the thanks,' declared Jimmy

James. 'Your video was a blast. We especially loved all the banter.'

What banter? There wasn't any. It was only me telling jokes. Maybe banter was American for jokes. Or maybe he'd come to the wrong house.

But there wasn't time to think about that terrible possibility as Jimmy James was busily answering all my parents' questions.

He told them how the actor selected for a small but key role as a typical British schoolboy had pulled out at the eleventh hour. So they had decided to find a typical British lad who didn't need any acting experience, just a personality that jumped off the screen.

Looking right at my parents, he said, 'We believe Louis could be that person. But we'd need to audition him next Thursday. I do realise how short notice that is. But we'd only need him for a morning at a hotel near Elstree. So what do you say, folks?'

Mum and Dad had plenty more to say – and fired zillions of questions at him – about the part, the film, and where it would be made (my scenes would be filmed in Winchester, this summer). On and on came the questions. All of which Jimmy answered patiently and with a genial smile, as if he were having the time of his life here.

In the middle of all this the real music teacher turned up. Well, Dad got rid of him in about five seconds flat and sped back.

Then Mum asked Jimmy James, 'Will you excuse us both for a moment? We need to talk about this.'

'Of course,' he said, waving his hands exuberantly. 'And please take as long as you like. I shall have a great time chatting to your two amazing sons.'

That's when I gave him Maddy's card.

'An agent based in California. Hmm,' he nodded, impressed.

'But she's only—' began Elliot.

'Only been based in California a short while,' I quickly interrupted. Let Jimmy James find out my agent is the same age as me later.

And then Mum and Dad came back. They weren't gone long, three minutes tops. I thought this was a very bad sign. I stood up too, shifting uneasily from foot to foot. Was my world about to collapse again?

Dad said, 'I apologise if we seem somewhat slow-witted but this has come as a complete surprise to us. We're disappointed Louis didn't feel he could share what he was doing with us, but ... some chances are too big to be ignored.

And we believe this opportunity is one of them.'

That's when I shouted, 'Mum, Dad, this is the coolest thing you've ever done,' and actually hugged them.

Jimmy James was on his feet too, vigorously shaking hands with my parents and asking them to sign something. He took some snaps of me too, said his team would be alerting the media (loved the way he said that) and then handed me a few lines of script to learn for Thursday.

He said, 'We'll also get you to do some improvisation – you and your buddy.' I realised he meant Edgar. 'Be so great to have him there as well,' said Jimmy James. 'Someone for you to bounce off.' Then he spoke into his phone, and moments later a black limo nearly as long as my entire road pulled up.

The chauffeur, holding an umbrella, leapt out and opened the rear door of the limo. As he was getting in, Jimmy James called out, 'Wonderful audition, Louis, and fabulous banter.'

Banter must mean jokes in America.

8.25 p.m.
No it doesn't.

Just had a very quick chat with Maddy. She was beyond thrilled, of course.

And she solved the mystery above.

It turns out Edgar didn't send any of the film of me telling jokes. Instead he spliced together all our arguments and posted that off. He also sent Maddy a copy.

'And you know what,' she said, 'I really think he was right. You and Edgar arguing was wonderfully funny—'

'While me telling jokes, which I'd practised for weeks and weeks, wasn't?' I interrupted.

'No, it wasn't quite as funny,' she said gently. 'In fact ...' She paused.

'Go on.'

'No, I don't want to say anything else.'

'Finish your sentence,' I urged.

'I don't think you'd be going to the audition if you'd just recited jokes.'

There was silence for a moment before I said, 'I have a horrible feeling you're right, Maddy. Which is awful, because it's going to make Edgar even more big-headed than he was before.'

Chapter Twenty-Two
Breaking the Spell

Friday March 21st
4.00 p.m.
I couldn't tell you one thing that happened at school today. I just strolled around in a happy daze. But then I've never had news like this before. That's probably why I still can't quite believe it.

4.30 p.m.
Maddy said I should tell Edgar the good news. I don't think he could have sounded more astonished if I'd announced I was to be the next James Bond.

'They've picked *you!*' His voice cracked

disbelievingly down the phone.

'And I've sort of got you to thank, it seems.'

'I merely saw how your interplay with me released your comic energy in an exciting, new way,' he replied, somewhat smugly.

Then I told Edgar that he had been invited along to the audition as well.

I expected him to scoff but instead he said, 'To be a small part of this next step in your career would please me greatly.'

A quick translation – Edgar's coming too. Should I be happy about that?

Probably not.

Saturday March 22nd

9.30 a.m.
Elliot just asked, 'That funny man who came round on Thursday – how do we know he wasn't just pretending he wanted Louis for a film? Maybe he's playing a big joke on us.'

'Did you see his car?' I demanded.

'He could have just hired that,' said Elliot.

'What about his card then?' I asked.

'What does that prove?' asked Elliot. 'You've got a flash card and you're not anybody famous.'

'Don't be jealous, Little Legs.'

Of course Elliot was babbling rubbish, but he

went on and on until Dad looked Jimmy James up on Wikipedia. There was a swanky press photo of him grinning from ear to ear on the red carpet at some movie premiere, and a list of all the films he's worked on. None of which I've seen or ever heard of – but still incredibly impressive. No wonder Mum and Dad kept studying it.

Sunday March 23rd

8.30 p.m.
Maddy has been watching me on Skype performing the lines I have to learn for Thursday. I'm telling this American girl about British schools. It's supposed to be funny but it really isn't. I don't think so anyway. Maddy agreed with me.

'Shall I try and improve this?' I asked.

'Best to wait until you get the part,' she said. 'Anyway, I believe it's a test to see if you can make something more hilarious than it really is.'

Maddy really understands show business.

Monday March 24th

7.30 p.m.
You know how Dunky put my mum and dad

under a spell? And I've tried everything to break it and failed every single time? I have the solution at last.

Be in a film.

The instant they discovered I'm going to be a movie star, Mum and Dad changed. And tonight they're so relaxed they're practically back to their old selves.

They have already rung up my school about Thursday and they are both taking time off work to come with me to the audition. When I'm famous I'll only remember the good times with them.

Tuesday March 25th

6.30 p.m.
The news of my audition has well and truly broken. My face is on the front page of the free newspaper (a picture Jimmy James took). And some of our neighbours have already called round. One lady even took a selfie with me. She said it was to show her grandchildren.

Wednesday March 26th

9.30 a.m.
History was made in assembly today. The Head

of Year offered me congratulations for being chosen to audition for a film tomorrow. He said he knew I would make the school proud!

Me! The most spectacularly useless pupil ever.

3.00 p.m.
Every kid in my class – and many others – is teeming around me, wanting to know every detail about tomorrow. You know what, my life feels bigger already.

6.25 p.m.
The word 'homework' hasn't passed my parents' lips once tonight. They are too busy gawping at my face in the local paper. At last I have made them proud.

7.00 p.m.
A final email confirming the details for tomorrow. A taxi will arrive at 6.15 a.m. (yes, 6.15 in the morning!), take me and 'my party' to the Langella Hotel near Elstree and then we will have breakfast with Jimmy James before my audition starts, in a hotel bedroom presumably. Which is a bit odd. Or maybe it isn't. I'm entering a whole new world.

8.25 p.m.

Performed my audition piece for the very last time on Skype for Maddy. She said I had really nailed it, and so wishes she could be there with me tomorrow for the most significant moment of my life. I so wish it too.

Instead I've got Edgar.

Chapter Twenty-Three
One Tiny Lie

Thursday March 27th

6.05 a.m.
Still not properly light, but Mum, Dad and yours truly are already downstairs (Elliot is away on a sleepover), and now Edgar has just turned up.

'Don't you look smart?' cooed Mum.

'Well, I felt a suit was called for,' said Edgar. 'And I'm wearing my shiniest black shoes.' He then said to me, 'I'm assuming my role is merely to sit in the background and observe.'

'Oh no,' I replied. 'They want you to join in the improvisation with me.'

Edgar immediately said, 'Right, take some

deep breaths.'

'I'm not nervous,' I said.

'I meant me.'

Then I saw a taxi pull up. 'Let's go,' I announced.

6.52 a.m.

On the way to Elstree now. Mum, Dad and Edgar are all looking incredibly tense. To help them unwind I tell some jokes. It's not long before Mum and Dad are laughing like crazed hyenas. Even Edgar joins in – once I've explained the meaning of the jokes to him. 'Ah yes, very droll in its simplistic way.'

6.58 a.m.

A text has just pinged in from Maddy – it must be about one o'clock in the morning for her – wishing me all the luck in the world. Then she went on: **Don't forget how very good – no, brilliant – you are**.

I so wish she was here with me now. Actually, I sort of feel she is.

7.48 a.m.

Waiting for us outside this huge hotel is a smartly dressed blond-haired woman brandishing a clipboard in one hand and a walkie-talkie in the other. She introduces herself as Alicia, Jimmy James's personal assistant. With a big beaming smile she adds, 'I know you are all going to have a fabulous time.' She sounds as if we've arrived here for our holidays.

She escorts us into a palatial lift and says, 'I'm sure you're ready for breakfast.' Actually, for the first time in my life I don't feel like eating anything. I just want to get on with the audition.

8.05 a.m.
Alicia leads us down this long corridor with cream walls, very expensive-looking mirrors and carpets so deep you practically have to wade through them. At the end is the breakfast room, where we're shown to a table by the window, which is flooded with early morning light.

'What a truly wonderful place to have breakfast,' whispers Mum.

It is busy already and everyone seems to be talking in hushed voices. Our waiter – a slightly stooped man with a very faint smile permanently etched on his face – speaks in such a low voice you have to strain to hear him.

We are all just tucking into a full English breakfast – Alicia practically insisted we have 'the works' – when a voice booms from the depths of the room, 'It's Louis the Laugh.'

'And it's Jimmy the boss,' I call back.

Beaming ferociously and wearing a panama hat, Jimmy James strides over to us. 'Hey, everyone,' he bellows as if addressing the whole hotel, 'I know we're going to have so much fun today.'

'I do wish people would stop saying that,' Edgar murmurs. 'It really puts me off.'

At that point Jimmy James stretches out a hand to Edgar. 'So glad your compatriot could join you.' He speaks as if Edgar and me are a double act. Yuk! And double yuk!

9.15 a.m.
At last we go up in the mirrored lift to the film company's suite on the first floor. We are escorted into their lounge first.

'Do make yourselves at home,' Alicia said to Mum and Dad. 'And would you like any more coffee or tea?'

'We're fine,' murmured Mum, obviously a bit disappointed she and Dad were being deposited here. They both hugged me and even got a bit misty-eyed. It's a new experience having my parents proud of me. I could get used to it.

'You've done extremely well,' said Dad.

'Now, just focus,' urged Mum.

We left them perched awkwardly on the edge

of a huge purple sofa, as Edgar and I followed Alicia and Jimmy into a room next door. There was no furniture save for a few chairs in the corner, but cables coiled all across the floor and two guys dressed completely in black were already setting up the cameras.

They ignored Edgar and me. In fact, they didn't talk to anyone and no one spoke to them. It was as if we were all pretending we couldn't see them. 'I fear I may need to use the facilities,' said Edgar.

'You'll be fine,' I growled. 'Just cross your legs – and don't, whatever you do, start thinking about fountains.'

Jimmy James settled down on a chair in the corner. His hat also merited a chair to itself. Alicia asked me solemnly, 'Are you ready to entertain?'

'Definitely,' I said, skidding towards my mark. Then Edgar was told to move next to me.

The cameras swept closer to us and Edgar actually shivered. What an amateur. 'Cameras are like giant black holes—' he began.

'Yeah, you can write a poem about it later,' I interrupted.

A very smiley girl popped up and dabbed a little bit of powder on my nose. Then she went over to Edgar. He shook his head firmly. 'I never

ever wear make-up.'

I grinned at the girl. 'He's so ugly nothing can help.'

9.50 a.m.
I finally got to perform my audition piece. Alicia just nodded at me and, wham, I was off – word perfect too. I didn't let the cameras zooming about all the time put me off. Or Edgar, who helpfully – not! – reminded me not to move my hands about just before I started.

After I finished there was silence. A young guy in yellow trousers, and also holding a clipboard, appeared. He was hovering in the corner of the room. But no one was looking at him. Every eye was fixed on Jimmy James, who'd been sitting completely motionless during my audition.

Finally he raised a finger and said, in a much quieter voice than usual, 'Could you do it again for us, Louis, but not quite so quickly?'

'I certainly could,' I said.

'Thank you very much, Louis.'

After I'd done this Jimmy James said softly, 'How about some improvisation now, lads?' He beckoned Edgar to come and stand beside me.

'Now, Edgar, you want to ask a girl out, but are not sure how to do it. So you have turned to Louis for help. I want you two just to have a conversation about that. And have fun, boys.'

Edgar frowned hard for a moment, and then said, 'Hey, dude, there's this brillo chick ...'

I started to laugh. 'Why are you talking like that?'

'I'm trying to sound like a typical teenager.'

Everyone was grinning now, even the cameramen.

'No one ever spoke like that in the history of the world,' I smiled. 'Just be yourself.'

Edgar considered. 'Er, Louis, there's this young damsel to whom I wish to plight my troth—'

'Which century are you in now?' I interrupted.

'Well, I do my best not to live in this one,' said Edgar.

That got a great booming laugh from Jimmy James. 'Now you're cooking with gas, boys. Carry on, be as eccentric as you like.'

'I don't suppose you'll struggle much with that, do you, Edgar?' I joked.

Edgar and I carried on arguing – or bantering – until finally I declared, 'You know what, Edgar, I give up with you. I'm better off playing stupid than playing Cupid,' and got a terrific laugh.

Then Jimmy James and Alicia whispered for a moment.

After which Jimmy James strode towards

Edgar and me and shook our hands again. 'We're so happy to have you here with us today, boys.'

'Very happy,' beamed Alicia.

'And what a memorable audition,' he said.

'Really fabulous,' agreed Alicia.

One more flash of blazing white teeth and they're both gone. The bloke in the yellow trousers exited too. We're left with the guys dismantling the cameras.

I looked at Edgar. 'Do you think they've gone to draw up my contract?'

'Hard to know,' replied Edgar, 'in this world of glued-on smiles.'

10.35 a.m.

It probably isn't that long until someone appears – but it feels like centuries. Then finally the guy in the yellow trousers pops up again. He comes over to us, smiling broadly.

'So, guys, have you enjoyed yourselves?' Up close he doesn't look very much older than Edgar and me. He has a very posh, plummy voice.

'Oh yeah,' I say. Edgar just stares at him.

'That's so brilliant, boys. Now would you like anything else to eat or drink? Go on, I'm sure you would. What would you like?'

'I would like you to answer a question please,' says Edgar. 'Who exactly are you?'

'Hey, I'm sorry. I'm Marky, Alicia's assistant.'

'And will Alicia and Jimmy James be returning soon?' asks Edgar.

'No, they've had to dash off to another meeting. You know how it is. Busy, busy people. But they so enjoyed spending time with you both.'

'And they liked my audition?' I ask eagerly – a bit too eagerly, actually.

'Oh, yeah,' says Marky.

'And will I be hearing from them?' I ask. (Too needy. I know.)

'Sure you will. Now I've got a surprise for you.'

I look at him extremely hopefully.

'You know your mum and dad have been next door. Well, they were able to watch every second of your audition on their own TV screen. What about that, boys?'

This is good, of course, but hardly the surprise I'm hoping for. I want them to say I'm so great I start filming tomorrow.

Still, my parents are very impressed by my audition. 'So natural and authoritative,' says Mum.

'Neither you nor Edgar seemed bothered by the cameras at all,' adds Dad.

Then, while Marky is sorting out our car home, Mum and Dad whisper excitedly to me, 'And did Jimmy James say anything to you?'

'He said it was a memorable audition and Alicia said it was fabulous.'

Dad nods eagerly, but I can tell he and Mum want much more than that.

And you know me, I always try and give my audience what it wants, so I continue, 'Well, there is something else but it's all hush-hush ...'

'Yes,' says Mum breathlessly. And both of them look so eager and hopeful I can't let them down.

So I announce, 'Jimmy James and the film company are working on my contract this very second.'

Edgar begins to splutter uncontrollably.

'So you have definitely got the part?' squeaks Mum.

'Oh yeah, I'm the one they want,' I say airily, ignoring Edgar's now very loud coughing. 'They are totally certain of that.'

Yes, all right, you could say I told them a tiny lie, but not for any bad reasons. I just wanted my mum and dad to start feeling good right away and not have to wait until I'm super sure.

So that's extremely kind of me, actually.

And come on, you're not going to tell someone their audition is 'memorable' and 'fabulous' and then not offer them the part, are you?

Chapter Twenty-Four
Your Local Film Star

Friday March 28th

4.00 p.m.
Everyone at my school went berserk the second I arrived today, with people yelling across the playground, 'Did you get it?'

And I yelled back, 'Of course, no problem.'

The news raced around the school. By break time I was surrounded by an army of pupils demanding to know exactly what film it is, and would they be able to see it in a cinema. And were any famous stars going to be appearing alongside me?

'No interviews today,' I cried. 'And please try

to treat me like a normal person, even though I'm now your local film star.'

9.05 p.m.
Quick chat with Maddy. I've even let her think the part is definitely mine. She asked more questions than my parents though, including, 'Did anyone actually say the role is yours?'

'No one said those actual words,' I admitted. 'But it was very strongly hinted.'

'I think I'd wait until they confirm it before you tell anyone,' said Maddy.

'What good advice,' I muttered.

But there wasn't a single person I knew who I hadn't already told.

I think Maddy would have asked me a lot more, but she seemed a bit distracted. Something was going on with her family. She didn't seem keen to go into details. Were her mum and dad going back on their promise that Maddy could come home every holiday, starting this Easter? I desperately hoped it wasn't that.

Saturday March 29th

10.00 a.m.
Mum and Dad have just sat down opposite me. But for once no lectures about homework, or

anything equally grisly.

Instead Dad said, 'We do realise you're the expert here, not us. So we just wondered what happens next, Louis?'

'Er, well, right now,' I said, 'Castel Films are busy working on the contract, which can take quite a while as they sort out terms and all that rhubarb.'

Dad nodded. 'Of course. We should have thought about that. And when the contract does arrive do you think we should ask a lawyer to look it over?'

'Er, sure. I guess that would be a good idea,' I said.

'And of course the lawyer will need to go over it very carefully, as we don't want them pressurising you into signing up for more than one film, do we?' said Mum.

'Don't we?' I queried.

'Louis,' cried Mum, 'your talent is very special and must be looked after so carefully.'

Yes, my mum really did say that last sentence. I tell you, my life is so brilliant right now, or it would be if … look, I'm convinced I'm in the film. Otherwise I wouldn't have told everyone I was. I mean, I'm not stupid.

But in a time when there are so many different forms of communication available, you'd think

Castel Films could have used one of them to put my mind at rest and just confirm the film part is mine.

So why haven't they done that?

Well, I think I've worked it out.

They don't believe it's necessary. They assume I know.

That's got to be the reason, hasn't it?

Come on, agree with me!

Please.

You know I'm right, don't you?

Sunday March 30th

7.30 p.m.

Waiting for Poppy to ring. And she just has.

'Oh, Louis, I stormed it tonight.'

'I knew you would.' She'd been appearing at her local theatre. Top of the bill too.

She said, 'Just before I went on I remembered those nasty messages again, but do you know what I did then?'

'No.'

'I thought of you, and straight away I started laughing.'

'Thanks. I think.'

'You really should be back on Noah and Lily's vlog. You're a top agony uncle.'

'You forget, they've got Grinning Gus now.'

'But he's all wrong for it,' protested Poppy. 'Still, what do you care? You're going to be a movie star now.'

'I sure am,' I beamed, with gleaming confidence. I'm absolutely certain Castel Films will get in touch tomorrow.

Monday March 31st

3.10 p.m.
My English teacher asked me to stay behind and said my latest essay showed definite signs of improvement. Now don't get too excited, I still only got a C+. But, as I'm normally in F territory, that's a dizzying rise.

And you know what, all through the day I kept looking at that grade in total wonderment. How on earth had I done that?

3.42 p.m.
I was just leaving school when a sixth former rushed up to me. He has never spoken to me in his life. But he introduced himself (Paul), then said he was an actor and reeled off his credits. After which he told me he would play any role – no matter how small – and he would be so grateful if I would inform the film company

191

about him. He has all this stuff on Instagram apparently which they can watch. He patted me on the back for several seconds as if I were his bestest mate in the entire world, then asked if I'd be meeting the director and the rest of the cast soon.

I said yeah, I'd see them all over the Easter holidays. Well, I might. You never know.

7.05 p.m.
But at home my doubts are running rampant. I'm sure I should have heard something by now. In the end only one thing settles my nerves. Doing homework.

I am certainly living in very strange times.

Tuesday April 1st

8.30 p.m.
No, still not a sausage from Castel Films.

What on earth is going on? This really is no way to treat a future film star.

Wednesday April 2nd

4.20 p.m.
Mum and Dad were both out when I got home today. They're watching Elliot in a school play

he's probably wrecking.

I'm relieved actually. Faking this 'I'm so happy' front all day at school and then at home is totally exhausting.

I even wonder if I should contact the film company myself. Maybe send them a merry little text saying, 'Hey, just checking, but I have got the part I auditioned for, haven't I?'

No, no, no!

I need to be far more subtle.

Maddy will know what I should say.

At this moment though, in faraway California, her mum will still be driving her to school. So I'll wait a few minutes. Actually I can't tell you how tired I am! I haven't been sleeping that well if you really want to know (which you don't).

So I'll take a very quick power nap first, and then call Maddy.

5.05 p.m.
Fell asleep right away and dreamt I was chatting to Maddy on Skype until she burst out of the screen, like some kind of superhero, which she sort of is. 'I can sort this,' she announced. 'So here's what you must do ...'

Dead annoyingly, that's when I woke up as someone was ringing the doorbell.

Talk about inconsiderate. Don't they realise

people are trying to sleep?

I opened the door, and then decided I must still be dreaming.

From out of the bright afternoon sunshine stepped ... Maddy.

Chapter Twenty-Five
Maddy Returns

5.10 p.m.

I gawped and gawped at her. 'But you're not due back for days and days yet ...'

'I know, but there was a chance to come home a bit earlier with Mum ... so here I am. Sorry,' said Maddy.

'What are you talking about? It's brilliant! Of course it is. Only I was just thinking of you – well, dreaming actually – and now here you really are. It's incredible.'

She'd cut her hair dead short, but it suited her and she was quite tanned as well. And I'd forgotten how sparkly her eyes were. I felt oddly shy for a moment. Then I gave her a massive hug.

'This is so great,' I began, but to be honest she looked a bit more doubtful. 'Is everything all right?' I asked.

'Not exactly.' She hesitated, then said mega-quickly, 'The thing is, Louis, I've got some bad news for you and some good news. Which would you like first?'

'The bad,' I replied at once. 'Get it over with.'

'OK,' she said.

We went into the kitchen and I said with a nervous laugh, 'Now you're looking incredibly serious. You're not going to tell me something bone-chillingly awful, are you?'

She laughed nervously too, and then speaking very fast again said, 'Castel Films have been in contact. You gave them my card and I suppose they thought I was the person to go to, and they said ...' Her voice fell away.

'I haven't got the part, have I?' I murmured.

Maddy's voice wasn't even a whisper. 'No ... I'm so sorry, Louis.'

It was such a horrible howling shock I couldn't bear to think about it. My mind went into meltdown and I began to gabble. 'Well, that's a blow, I'd even made a start on my Oscar speech. Did they say why? Was I too handsome maybe? This happens to me a lot. People say it's

196

just not realistic to cast someone who looks like a model.' Suddenly I burst out, 'I made them laugh, Maddy, and in fact they nearly killed themselves laughing.'

'I know, and they liked you so much but ...'

'But?' I echoed.

'They've completely rethought the part.'

'I see ...' Then I let out a massive yowl, as if I'd just cut my hand or something. 'Sorry about that sound effect,' I said to Maddy, who was looking dead concerned now, 'but I'm more disappointed than I've ever been in my entire life.'

'I know,' she said, 'and go on making as many funny noises as you like.'

'No, I think I'm finished for now, thanks.' I slumped down behind the table.

Maddy sat beside me and squeezed my hand tightly. Neither of us spoke for several seconds.

Then she said, 'I didn't want to tell you on the phone, so I waited until ...'

'I appreciate that.' Then I leapt up. 'So they've rethought the part. That's OK. I can change. Be someone else. They just tell me what they want, and I'll be that person. Easy ... but they've got to let me audition again, haven't they?'

'Er ... y-e-a-h,' she said, incredibly slowly.

'That's a no, then?'

'The thing is, they've already decided who

they want.'

'That was quick.'

Her face reddened. 'Actually, they've offered it to someone you know.'

'Really ...' I thought for a moment. 'It's Noah, isn't it? Got to be.'

'No ...'

'Tell me it's not Grinning Gus.'

'It's not Grinning Gus. Actually, and you won't believe this ... they've offered it to my other client.'

I was so massively shocked I couldn't speak at first. 'Edgar! They've offered my role to Edgar! But why?'

Maddy lowered her head. 'Well, they decided a typical British boy is actually a geek. And so they said ...'

'Go on,' I demanded.

'Edgar has a core innocence and geekiness that seems real,' she said quickly.

'I can't believe it! Edgar! Edgar in a film.' Then I laughed. 'Well, good for him.'

'Do you mean that, Louis?'

'Yeah, I'm not bitter – well, I am. But he'll either be completely amazing or totally terrible.'

'I know.'

'Do Castel Films have any idea what they are taking on?' I grinned.

'No,' laughed Maddy.

'I bet he's shocked – but excited too. Not that he'll admit that.'

'I haven't told him yet,' said Maddy.

'Well, let him know that I'm pleased for him. Or I will be,' I added. 'I suppose that's the good news you mentioned.'

Maddy hesitated, and then looked extremely embarrassed. 'Yeah, that's right.'

'You'd better go and tell Edgar then.'

'Really?'

'Yeah. It's great we're keeping it in the agency at least,' I said.

'You want to be on your own, don't you?'

Trust Maddy to realise that.

'Only for a bit, and then I'll have to tell everyone the truth. What fun!'

'I'd wait until tomorrow,' said Maddy.

'Would you?'

'Yeah, start with your parents tomorrow night.'

'You're right,' I said. 'Give them one more day thinking their son's going to be a movie star.'

'I'm not giving up,' said Maddy. 'And you mustn't either.'

I gave a small smile. 'OK.'

'No, I mean it, Louis, I'll never give up.'

7.40 p.m.

My grandparents had just popped round to congratulate me on my film role and I was giving a superb acting performance of being happy – when the doorbell rang. And there, demanding to see me, was Edgar.

'I'm absolutely furious,' he began. 'How dare they offer me your—'

'Keep your voice down. I haven't told anyone yet.'

'I'm sorry, but I'm hopping mad,' said Edgar. 'I have just signed a contract with the local newspaper to produce a new poem every week for the next six months. I am also putting together material for my first poetry collection. So the idea that I would drop all that to appear in some trashy film—'

'You don't want to do it?' I interrupted.

'Of course I don't. And I'm insulted they even asked me. Somehow I managed to send them a remarkably restrained email. I thought you might appreciate seeing a copy.'

Incredulously, I read:

Dear Sir,

Thank you for your offer of a performing role in your upcoming cinematic production, which I know you meant kindly. As I believe my agent has already made clear, I am far too busy to consider your proposition. Apart from my academic studies, I am a poet, whose reputation is growing rapidly. I would advise you to instead cast my friend, Louis.

'I wrote "friend",' Edgar said, 'as I thought it would carry more weight.'

I nodded and read on.

He has a very real talent for this sort of light, glib nonsense. So I would strongly recommend you to contact him at your earliest convenience.
Yours most faithfully,
Edgar

I shook my head. 'Are you sure you don't want to be in a film. I mean, a chance like this …'

'Perfectly sure,' interrupted Edgar.

'And you're not doing it out of a loyalty to me?'

'Certainly not,' he spluttered.

'Well, that's lucky. Because from what Maddy has told me they've rethought the role – so there's no way they're going to offer it to me instead.'

'Then they're making a big mistake. That rubbish suits you perfectly.'

I grinned suddenly. 'Cheers, Edgar, I appreciate that. By the way,' I went on, 'will it be all right if I pop round sometime soon and take a peek at your collection of rocks?'

'Of course,' said Edgar, looking very surprised but pleased. 'You can see how I've now colour-coded all my rocks, if you like,' he added enticingly.

'I definitely would like.'

Edgar smiled a bit awkwardly at me. 'Excellent. Well ... call round anytime you wish, Louis. I'm always at home.'

Thursday April 3rd

7.05 p.m.
All day the news from Castel Films has been hanging over me like my own personal storm cloud. I thought one of my parents might have noticed I wasn't as happy as I was pretending to be. But they haven't. I really am a good actor.

I can't put if off any more, though. This is it. I'm not even going to try to fool my parents this time. That never really works anyway. Instead I'm going to try something entirely different.

I'm going to tell them, and everyone else, the awful truth.

But never in a million, trillion years have I dreaded anything so much.

Chapter Twenty-Six
Going Viral

7.58 p.m.
I bounced into the living room, where Mum and Dad were waiting for me (I'd asked if I could tell them something) and, unfortunately, Elliot as well.

Poor Mum and Dad looked so excited.

'This is to let you know, the film company have been in contact,' I began ...

'Come on, get on with it and stop showing off,' demanded Elliot.

I laughed bitterly to myself.

That's when the doorbell rang.

Elliot groaned. Dad answered it, and in sped a breathless Maddy.

'Maddy!' cried Mum. 'Have you broken up for the Easter holidays already?'

'Er yes,' said Maddy vaguely.

'Well, welcome home,' chorused Mum and Dad.

'Thanks,' said Maddy even more vaguely, and then turned to me. 'I'm not too late ... you haven't told them?'

'Just going to now,' I said.

'Well, I'll do it.'

'No, Maddy, it's fine.' It was typical of her to come to my rescue. Only this time I didn't need rescuing. 'I'm handling this.'

'No, Louis, I am.' When she wants to, Maddy can be a pretty awe-inspiring presence. And this was one of those occasions. 'I am your agent,' she added, smiling sweetly at me before turning to my parents. 'As you know, Louis was forced to resign from Noah and Lily's vlog.'

Mum and Dad shifted about more than a bit awkwardly, while I wondered why on earth Maddy was bringing that up now. 'What you don't know – in fact, what even Louis doesn't know, and I only discovered today, is that Noah and Lily's followers have been demanding Louis's return. I ran off some of their comments for you.'

Very briskly, as if she were passing round the

minutes of a meeting, she handed my parents pages and pages of comments about me.

Mum and Dad started reading them aloud in highly, bewildered voices:

'"I love the way Louis laughs with people but never at them. He must return immediately."

'"I want to be in Louis's world. He always lifts my spirits."

'"I'm so missing Louis's enthusiasm and infectious fun."

'"Louis is my friend and I miss him so much. When is he coming back?"'

Finally they stopped reading and looked right at me.

'There are many, many more,' said Mum. She sounded amazed. Well, so was I.

'Now an online petition has started,' Maddy said, 'for you to return.'

'You're joking ...' I cried.

'And it's already gone viral,' continued Maddy triumphantly.

Mum shook her head in wonderment.

'Today,' continued Maddy, 'I had a long conversation with Noah and Lily. Grinning Gus has gone. In fact, he only lasted one week.'

'He must be even more annoying than you,' chirped Elliot.

'They tried other friends from the YouTube

community. Big names. But none of them could replace you, Louis.'

'I know,' I murmured.

'By the way,' Maddy's voice rose slightly. 'Noah and Lily are sorry they never contacted you. But they explained to me that being in the public eye means they have to be extremely careful what they do. And the truth is, they were banned from having anything to do with you by your mum and dad.'

'I wish *I* was,' muttered Elliot, while Mum and Dad shifted about even more awkwardly.

Then Maddy turned and smiled at me. 'But Noah and Lily are desperate for you to return.'

The smile on my face was growing bigger too. But then I stopped and looked at my parents. Maddy was staring right at them too.

'Sometimes,' said Dad, 'you can make bad decisions for the best of reasons.'

This sounded hopeful.

'After your parents' evening,' Dad continued, 'we worried we weren't doing the best for you. We know comedy and performing is your thing, Louis. But we were very keen for you to discover other talents too. We felt we owed you that. It was part of our job, if you like. Only we realise now that we shouldn't have stopped you appearing on that vlog.'

'Wow!' cried Elliot. 'You're admitting you did something wrong. Parents never ever do that.'

'Well, these parents are doing it now,' said Mum. 'We focused too much on the things *we* think are important. Just because vlogging isn't part of our world. Well, this seems the perfect moment for the ban to be lifted.'

'So you may return to your waiting public, Louis,' smiled Dad. 'I would just point out, though, that you are going to be extremely busy with your vlogging *and* a film role.'

'I agree,' said Maddy. 'And that's why I have pulled Louis out of the film part. It was only a very small role but it would have taken up a huge amount of time. And in the future Louis won't just appear in a few minutes of the vlogs ...'

'You've cancelled the film,' gasped Dad.

'Yes, I have,' said Maddy fearlessly. 'As an agent it's my job to do what is best for my clients.'

I saw exactly what Maddy was doing here. She was on a face-saving mission. For me. The good news about Noah and Lily meant she could get away with it too. My family need never know the awful truth.

But I couldn't let her do this, especially as Mum and Dad and Elliot were looking at her so angrily.

'You really can't do this, Maddy,' said Mum in a tight, furious voice, 'not without consulting anyone.'

'I've already done it,' said Maddy airily.

What an agent! What a girlfriend! But I chipped in, 'Maddy hasn't done anything except try to protect me. Actually, the film company have made a truly catastrophic error of judgement and decided they don't want me.'

'What?' chorused Mum and Dad, looking utterly bewildered.

'Sorry – I didn't mean to mislead you,' I said. 'I really thought the part was in the bag, but it wasn't.'

'Because they've totally rethought the role,' added Maddy.

'And instead they've offered the part to that awesome force known as Edgar,' I explained.

'Edgar,' spluttered Mum. 'Your Edgar.'

'The very same. Only he's turned it down.'

'I'll do it,' piped up Elliot. 'I've been in five school plays now.'

'And rubbish in every one of them,' I said.

'How long have you known this, Louis?' demanded Mum.

'Since yesterday. I was trying to pick the right moment to tell you.'

There was silence for a moment before Dad

declared, 'Well, from what I've read, film roles can be cut to nothing in the editing room. But to be on a vlog, now that's much more special.'

'And every single week too,' said Mum. 'Just wait until I tell the people at work. Every one of their kids is mad about the YouTubers, as I think you call them.'

'And the film would probably have flopped anyhow,' said Elliot.

Yes, my family can be a massive pain – but there are a few moments when they totally come through for you. And being with them is the best place in the world to be.

Chapter Twenty-Seven

The Best News of All

8.11 p.m.

After a few minutes Maddy got up. 'I'll be off then.'

'Where are you staying, Maddy?' asked Mum.

Funny, I hadn't thought to ask her.

'In my old house,' said Maddy, so casually that it didn't register at first.

Then it did, and my head was a whirl. 'But how? How are you able to live there again?'

Everyone was staring at her but Maddy said hyper-casually, 'I was really homesick in America, and so was Mum. But Dad, it turned out, was the most homesick of us all. He missed everything. And so ...' She paused.

'Go on,' I cried urgently.

'He's been talking about relocating back for a while. That's what all the hassle was about. But I didn't tell you before, just in case it didn't happen. But now he's finally decided ...'

'Ye-e-e-s!' I yelled.

'And as our house hadn't been rented out yet, we can move straight back in. Mum's come home with me. Dad's still in America for now as he has to ...'

But I stopped listening after that. I'd heard the important part. *MADDY IS BACK HOME FOR GOOD.*

I've got to write that again – only much bigger.

MADDY IS BACK HOME FOR GOOD.

At the doorway I said to her, 'That was the good news you meant to tell me yesterday, wasn't it – not Edgar being offered my part?'

She nodded. 'But you were so down about the film that I thought nothing can make up for that, so I decided to wait and tell you another time.'

I shook my head incredulously. 'Sometimes, Maddy, you are totally insane. That's the only explanation. Don't you realise that you coming home makes up for twenty lost film parts? I can get through anything now – including telling the entire school that I won't be popping up at the local cinema after all. In fact, I won't even notice that now you are—'

'Don't say another word,' interrupted Maddy fiercely, 'because you're making me cry.'

8.20 p.m.
My parents were saying how tomorrow night we weren't going to do anything except chill, have a good family meal together, and then watch whatever Elliot and I wanted.

Yes, they were exactly like dream parents again.

So I thought it would be OK if I finally told them about my C+ in English, which I was a teeny bit proud of actually. Of course they demanded to see it. And they gazed at the unfamiliar grade for as long as I had.

Then Mum asked gently, 'And Edgar didn't do this for you?'

'Mum, Edgar would have got a triple A at least. This was all my unaided work.'

Suddenly a great beam of a smile burst onto Mum's face. 'Now you see, Louis, what we were trying to do. We just wanted to make sure you didn't write yourself off at school, and that with some extra effort ... actually I'm sure you could get C+ in many other subjects too.'

'Maybe even a B,' declared Dad.

'If not an—' began Mum.

'Don't even say it,' I shrieked.

Oh no. What have I done?

9.50 p.m.

Maddy rang with a strange request. She asked if I'd like to go for a walk. Normally I can't think of anything more boring. My relatives always go for a stroll on Christmas Day afternoon and I always try and get out of it.

But tonight I said, 'You know what, I really would.'

There wasn't a star in the sky as we strolled hand-in-hand round the dullest village in the known universe. And it was totally and completely brilliant.

We talked about everything. The film. Noah and Lily. America. It was so awesome that Maddy was home again. Then finally Maddy said, 'You returning to Noah and Lily's vlog is only the start, Louis. There are so many more exciting things ahead for us. I can just sense it.'

'You know what? So can I. And it'd be so great to tell you what does happen next. Only I've totally run out of space.

So instead I'll bow very low and thank you for ... well, you know, you've been my best ever audience.

That's why I so hate saying goodbye to you.

Smile on!

Your friend,

Louis the Laugh

LOUIS THE LAUGH RETURNS!
The brilliantly funny sequel to
My Parents Are Driving Me Crazy

ISBN 978-1-78270-172-9

What can you do when you're trapped
in a TECHNOLOGY TIME WARP?
When Louis's parents decide he spends
too much time "glued to screens" they
come up with their WORST IDEA EVER –
a TOTAL BAN on tablets, computers
and mobiles! Louis needs a plan to
FIGHT BACK, and FAST!
Can his best friend Maddy come
to the RESCUE?

Pete Johnson Facts
www.petejohnsonauthor.com

Pete's favourite subjects at school were English and History. His least favourite was Maths.

He has a West Highland terrier called Hattie.

Pete has always loved reading. When he was younger he would read up to six books a week – even more in the school holidays!

His most favourite book as a child was *One Hundred and One Dalmatians*. He wrote to the author, Dodie Smith, and she encouraged him to become a writer.

Other childhood favourites include *The Witches* by Roald Dahl, *Tom's Midnight Garden* by Philippa Pearce and Enid Blyton's *The Mystery of the Invisible Thief*.

When he was younger, Pete used to sleepwalk. One night he woke up in his pyjamas walking along a busy road.

His favourite food is chocolate. He especially loves Easter eggs!

He loved to watch old black and white movies with his dad on Saturday night and used to review films on Radio 1. Sometimes he watched three films in a day! Pete has met lots of famous actors and collects signed film pictures.

Pete likes to start writing by eight o'clock in the morning. He reads all his books out loud to see if the dialogue sounds right. And if he's stuck for an idea he goes for a long walk.

Wherever he goes, Pete always carries a notebook with him. The best ideas come when you're least expecting them, he says. Why don't you try that too? Maybe you'll have a brilliant idea for your own book!

The Great
Louis the Laugh Quiz!

How well do you know *How to Fool Your Parents*?
Take our fiendish quiz and find out!

1   What does Louis do in Mr Duncan's (Dunky's)
    lesson that gets him into so much trouble?
2   Where has Maddy moved away to?
3   Edgar's nan mistakes Louis for someone else.
    Can you remember his name? (A very tough
    question, so here's a clue: it begins with T.)
4   What are the names of the vloggers whose
    show Louis appears on?
5   Louis's parents decide the whole family is
    going to learn to play a musical instrument.
    Which one?

6 Who does Louis call to ask them to do his homework for him?

7 Who is Grinning Gus?

8 Castel Films sends someone to Louis's house. Who is it?

9 What is the name of Louis's new friend whose mum believes in 'Yes Parenting'?

10 What amazing grade does Louis get for his homework at the end of the story?

*   *   *

A Note from Pete

A huge thank you to all the book clubs who have been in contact. I am thrilled that my books are so popular with you.

Anyone can start a book club, and they are great fun. So here are a few suggestions of what you might like to think about, just to get you going. (Of course you don't have to be in a book club – you can do it just for fun!)

What do you think of the book's title?

- Did it grab your interest right away?
- The original title of the book was *How to Trick Your Parents*. Was it right to change it?
- If you could give the book another title what would it be?

Parents' evening

- These are not usually hilarious events. How does Louis make it funny? Look at what he says ('You can either go and visit a man with a face like a decaying potato ...') and also his comic reactions. (For example: 'I am in quite a lot of torment, what with me still swallowing gallons of blood and feeling incredibly weak.')

What exactly has happened to Louis? How much is he exaggerating?

- Has anything funny ever happened to you at a parents' evening?

The secret

- Maddy says there is a practically foolproof way to fool parents. What do you think of it?
- Why doesn't it work for Louis? Would it work for you?
- Do you have any tips on how to encourage parents to do what you want?

Edgar

- 'I will admit, even Edgar needs a friend. But that person could never be me.' Why does Louis say this?
- How does his opinion of Edgar change? Did your opinion alter as well?
- Would you like Edgar as a friend?
- Apart from Louis, who are your favourite characters – Maddy, Poppy, Elliot, Edgar, Noah and Lily? Why?

Yes Parenting

- We meet Jack in this story whose mum never likes to say 'no' to him or his sister, Maisie.
- What do you think of Yes Parenting?

- Would you like it if your parents didn't said 'no' to you for a whole day?
- How is this idea treated in the story?"

Nasty messages
- Poppy is a talented conjuror who has her own website. Most people leave her 'really lovely' messages, but some put up stuff that upsets her. If Poppy were your friend, what would you say to her?
- How does Louis try to help her?
- Do you think it is good that this subject appears in a story?

What did you most enjoy about *How to Fool Your Parents*?
- Many readers pick comic scenes – such as when Louis goes to school in his pyjamas. Was this a favourite of yours too?
- Some readers see Louis as a 'friend'. Do you? Is he like you at all – or maybe one of your friends?
- Do you think the story would make a cool film? Who would you cast as Louis and Maddy?
- If you could portray one character from this story, who would it be?